GRANNY GETS FANCY

A SECRET AGENT GRANNY MYSTERY BOOK 6

HARPER LIN

This is a work of fiction. Names, characters, organizations, places, events, and incidents are either products of the author's imagination or are used fictitiously.

GRANNY GETS FANCY

ISBN: 978-1-987859-67-6

www.harperlin.com

ONE

It was a terrible waste of a lovely knife.

The knife was sterling silver, with one of those highly ornate handles that was all elaborate scroll-work and fluting and floral designs, making it resemble some Baroque masterpiece. It would have graced even the most elegant table.

It did not look lovely stuck in the back of a paunchy old drunk.

I'm Barbara Gold. Age: seventy. Height: five foot five. Eyes: blue. Hair: gray. Weight: none of your business. Specialties: Undercover surveillance, small arms, chemical weapons, Middle Eastern and Latin American politics. Current status: Retired CIA agent, widow, and grandmother.

Addendum to current status: Relapsing into boredom after one of the high points of my life.

At least until that knife got ruined.

Perhaps I should back up.

It was a couple of days before, the paunchy drunk was still alive, the silver steak knife was cutting into the flesh of creatures further down the food chain, and I was having lunch with my boyfriend, Octavian.

We were at the Tic Toc Café, one of Cheerville's more popular, and annoying, lunch spots. Popular because they made crepes to die for, annoying because every wall was covered with clocks of all descriptions—grandfather clocks, antique cast iron clocks taken from old railway stations, cuckoo clocks, you name it. They all ticked and tocked while we had to raise our voices to be heard. If it weren't for those crepes—and a cheese-cake I would never tell my doctor I ordered—I would never come here.

Octavian was an added incentive, of course. A dashing gentleman of my age, with dapper style—jacket and tie almost every day, usually in summer colors no matter what the season—a friendly demeanor, and better teeth than many a man half his age, he had been my boyfriend for several months now.

Yes, a pair of seventy-year-olds were dating. Surprised? You shouldn't be. We had both lost our beloved spouses, both gone through a dark period of mourning and loneliness and despair, both pulled ourselves up by our bootstraps, and both started living life again. Doing that was essential. The worst thing you could do when you got to the wrong side of retirement age was give up. Through my CIA training, I had learned not to give up. Octavian had learned it through more peaceful means, but he had learned it. The man had quite a bit of inner strength.

"Lovely crepes," Octavian said, taking another bite of his lunch. "As sweet as you are, my dear."

"Don't be silly," I said, giggling like a schoolgirl. He had that effect on me.

"What are you doing Friday night?" he asked.

"I have no plans at the moment."

"Would you like to go to a formal dinner? It's a charity function for the Cheerville Hospital's children's wing. I go every year."

"Well, that sounds like a good cause."

"It is," he said, nodding, "and it's quite the extravaganza. Formal wear, fine dining, fashion show, charity auction. The works. I'll treat you."

"If it's for charity, you don't have to treat me."

"It's five hundred dollars a plate."

I blinked then shrugged. I had just received a ridiculous amount of money for playing a small part in a movie. Saving the star from several murder attempts had perhaps added to my pay scale. "I don't mind," I said.

He pointed his fork at me. "Oh yes, Little Miss Moneybags. I haven't forgiven you for getting to act beside Cliff Armstrong."

I couldn't help letting out a lovelorn sigh. Not a polite thing to do in front of your boyfriend. Every woman in the country swooned over that action hero, as did every gay man. Every straight man—that would include Octavian, by the way—looked up to him as the epitome of manly prowess.

"Humph," Octavian added.

"Dreamy" was all I said. I hadn't meant to say it out loud.

"All right, we can go Dutch."

That was the only time a crush on a movie star had cost me five hundred dollars.

So on Friday, I picked out a lovely red dress—a color I didn't realize would become all too appropriate for the occasion—a pair of matching shoes, some pearls, and a gold watch. I rarely dressed up so much. When I was younger, I was more of a T-shirt-and-jeans girl or a combat-boots-and-camouflage girl when I was on duty. But I could smarten up when I needed to.

Octavian beat me, though. He showed up at my house in a spotless tuxedo.

That tuxedo became slightly less spotless as soon as I opened the door for him.

Dandelion, my tortoiseshell kitten, shot out from her hiding place under the couch and whooshed like a furry little meteor across the living room to attach herself to Octavian's leg.

I pried her off claw by claw, leaving little marks and a fair amount of fur on his pants leg.

"Oh dear," I said.

"Don't worry. It's a rental."

"That's worse! That means you won't get your security deposit back."

"Oh dear," Octavian said. He hadn't thought of that.

Dandelion scrabbled in my hands, trying to claw at my dress. The red seemed to attract her. Perhaps she thought she was a bull in Spain. She obviously didn't know the fate of most Spanish bulls.

We escaped my house before Dandelion could do any more damage, and we drove in Octavian's car over to the Cheerville Country Club.

I'd never been inside, and Octavian wasn't a member either. He had done quite well in the stock market in his younger years and would certainly have been welcome, but he said he didn't like the crowd.

"Too snooty," he said as we pulled up a long, arching driveway to what looked like a plantation from some Civil War movie. "I like to spend my time with real people. They're more interesting."

"Careful what you wish for," I said.

We laughed. Octavian was the only person in town besides the police chief who knew that I had worked for the CIA. I hadn't intended to tell him, but my getting kidnapped by gangsters and spirited away in a miniature submarine had clued him in that I was a little more than a sweet old lady who doted on her cat and grandson.

I also learned that he was a bit more than a kindly retired businessman who retained a spark of life. He had held up remarkably well during all the gunplay and had even helped get us saved by the police.

We pulled up in front, behind a line of cars that were far more expensive than Octavian's. Soon a young man in a white sports coat with the country club's crest on it welcomed us, ushered us out, and parked the car for Octavian.

Octavian hooked an arm around mine, and we ascended the stone steps then passed between the columns and through the broad front door along with the flow of the crowd. Everyone was smartly dressed—tuxedos or tailored business suits for the men, evening dresses for the ladies. I smelled expensive perfume, high-end cologne, and a mixture of old and new money.

We passed over a plush red carpet and into a huge dining hall with a vaulted ceiling and columns decorated with gold leaf. We checked our tickets to see where we were seated and found ourselves near the back.

"Oh well," Octavian said with a shrug. "It's because we only paid five hundred dollars each."

"Only?"

"If you pay more, you get better seats."

We sat. Each place had a program. Reading through it, I found we were going to be entertained by a children's chorus, a local comedian, the firefighters' chorus—be still my heart—and a fashion show. The menu had a meat option and a vegetarian option. Five hundred bucks and I didn't even get to choose from a full menu?

Octavian leaned over to me.

"When I lived in the city, I used to donate to the Metropolitan Children's Hospital. Their fundraisers were even bigger, as you can imagine. We also took the kids on outings, at least the ones who could go. The zoo, the movies, that sort of thing. For those too sick to move, we paid for magicians and clowns to come into the ward."

"You seem very dedicated to this cause."

A shadow passed over Octavian's face.

"Yeah. I have been all my life. There was a kid in my class at school, Charley Rains. He got leukemia and died."

"Oh dear. How old was he?"

"Fourteen."

I put a hand on his. It was obvious that it had really affected him when he was young, and the memory affected him still. My career had made me see a lot of death, but it was always ugly. A child's death was even uglier.

Before I could say anything, another couple sat at our table. He wore a yellow plaid suit that was far too loud and cheap for the occasion. She wore an equally loud and cheap dress and far too much makeup. They were of middle age, and both had on flashy jewelry that looked expensive but lacked taste.

After a moment, I recognized them.

"Hello," I said. "You're—"

Both shot out their hands to shake mine.

"Peter and Penny Price, the used-car king and queen!" they said in unison.

They had cheesy local commercials on late-night television. I'd never been to their used-car lot, but I had seen it several times—a huge expanse near the freeway that must have had hundreds of vehicles. Apparently, the used-car business had been kind to them, judging from the emeralds and rubies that grated against my fingers as I shook their hands.

They withdrew their hands then extended them again, this time holding business cards. I hadn't seen them get the cards out of their pocket or purse. They had just appeared. A nice sleight of hand. Peter offered me a card while Penny offered one to Octavian. We glanced at each other and took them, not knowing what else to do.

"Remember," Peter said, "the price is always perfect ..."

"...when you deal with a Price!" Penny finished.

It was the punchline from their commercials. They flashed two sets of perfect teeth at us. Instinctively, Octavian flashed back his own teeth. His teeth were not perfect but were surprisingly white and straight for his age. Even better, they were real.

Octavian: one. Used-car salesmen: zero.

We were saved from further conversation by another couple sitting down at our table, who immediately got subjected to the same treatment. The man, who had the meticulously clean hands of someone in the medical profession, made the mistake of mentioning he liked their commercials. That got him targeted with a hard-line sales pitch.

They, in turn, were saved by our emcee for the evening, standing up at a lectern on the stage at the front of the room and welcoming us all there. The lights went down, and waiters began to serve drinks and take our orders.

There followed a boring and seemingly endless speech by the emcee, who was also the president of the country club. While I was sure this fellow was quite successful in whatever career he'd had before spending his retirement running a country club, he was not an engaging speaker. After five minutes of telling us how we needed to help sick children, as if we hadn't already figured that out, he moved on to golf jokes.

Golf jokes.

Apologies to anyone out there who likes golf, but if there was anything that bored me more than golf, it was men talking about golf. I would rather watch my grandson play video games. I would rather wash the dishes. I would rather go to the bathroom.

The bathroom! Ah, that sanctuary for women who wanted to get away from dull male conversation. That was what I needed to do. I needed to go to the bathroom. I could hide in there until the golf jokes were over. Women could spend ages in the bathroom and guys never questioned what we did in there. We called it female privilege.

"I have to go to the bathroom," I whispered to Octavian.

"Lucky girl," he grumbled. "These golf jokes are going to go on forever."

I stood. So did Penny Price.

"I have to go to the bathroom too," she whispered.

Oh well. I guessed I couldn't save myself from boring female conversation. At least she hated golf as much as I did.

We tiptoed to the back of the room, as much as one could tiptoe in heels. One of the waiters gestured down a hallway, guessing our intent. A small crowd of women was already heading down there. I looked back and saw several more women following.

I doubted the speaker cared, assuming he'd noticed. The golf jokes weren't for us, anyway.

The ladies' room was at the end of a long hallway, past the coat check and the men's room.

"We're in luck," Penny said. "There's already a line."

Indeed there was. That meant we got a longer

reprieve from the speech. Maybe by the time I got back, the children's chorus would be warbling through a song and there would be some food on the table.

Penny started glad-handing all the people in line, doing her sleight of hand to produce her business cards and talking about how she and her husband offered discounts to anyone who was at the fundraiser, as if anyone who put down five hundred dollars for a meal at a charity dinner would buy a used car.

Penny was wearing a sleeveless gown, so the magic trick was doubly impressive. I had to watch her do it several times before I caught how she managed. She would shake hands, which brought the eye of the other person either level to make eye contact or down to look at the hand, then she would lean back, saying something while gesturing with her hand over her head. That brought the eye up. Then she would lean forward, which automatically got the person to make eye contact.

That was when her hand would go down, slip a card out of an unobtrusive side pocket in her purse, turn to hide the card, then reveal it with a flourish. The last time her target had been looking at her hand, it had been open and over her head, so they got a jolt, thinking the card had appeared out of nowhere.

Pretty impressive. There was more to Peter and Penny Price than flashy jewelry and eager sales pitches.

There was more than met the eye in the men's room too. It was a pity I wasn't paying more attention to that door than to my companion's hand.

Because just as Penny was about to do her little trick on yet another unwilling subject, a man came running out of the men's bathroom, his belt unbuckled, his shirt half in and half out, and a trail of toilet paper sticking out of the back of his pants, undulating in the air behind him like a long white tail.

"Help!" he shouted. "A man's been killed!"

"Here we go again," I muttered. "Five hundred bucks for a meal, and I don't even get to eat it."

TWO

Of course, the first thing I did was enter the men's room.

This was the first time I had entered a men's bathroom since sixth grade, when Amanda Prager and Dolores Samson had dared me to go into the boys' room at our school. I was a sucker for dares. There hadn't been any boys in the bathroom that time, but our principal had been waiting for me in the hall when I came out.

There was no danger of Saturday-morning detention this time, but there was a boy in the bathroom.

Well, a grown man with a silver knife stuck in his back.

Thankfully, he lay facedown in front of the urinals, his hands still down near his waist.

I say "thankfully" because he had obviously been using the urinal when he had been stabbed in the back. I knew this because there were two puddles around him, one of blood and the other of, well, you know.

This was exactly what I was afraid I would see back in sixth grade, minus the knife and blood and everything.

My first reaction was to duck down, knees protesting, and look under the stalls. I didn't see anyone in there.

I stood, both knees popping, and moved down the row of stalls. All were open. At the end was an open area with the urinals along one wall and a row of sinks on the other. I saw nothing on the floor.

I hurried back to the stalls, knowing I had only moments before I got interrupted.

I didn't go to the victim, but I saw that the knife had been planted up to the hilt in his back, just to the left of the spine. I suspected it had hit the heart, judging from how much the blood had spread. An initial spray, powered by one of the last heartbeats this poor fellow ever had, had shot out and bathed the wall in a livid streak.

A second heartbeat had squirted more blood from around the knife, but it hadn't reached as far and was visible only as a line extending on the floor a few inches beyond the pool of blood.

If there had been a third heartbeat, it had been a weak one and hadn't projected any blood farther than the pool had reached. From that point on, he was dead, the blood slowly leaking out of the wound.

But the pool was pretty big. He had been dead for a minute or two, while the man with the toilet paper tail had run out less than twenty seconds ago.

The victim was what one would charitably call "stout." Uncharitably, you would say he had a beer gut the size of Baltimore. What I could see of his face was florid, with a big red nose scarred from habitual heavy drinking.

I needed to check those stalls for evidence. There was nothing I could do for that poor man on the floor.

The first stall had nothing.

As I moved to the second stall, I heard an approaching clamor in the hallway. Uh-oh. Time was almost up.

The second stall hadn't been flushed. Yuck. I did a quick scan and saw nothing.

I got to the third stall just as the men's room door opened.

One of the young attendants with the country club logo on his blazer saw me, yelped, and slammed the door. "I'm so sorry, ma'am!" he called out. "I thought this was the men's room."

I entered the third stall. Nothing on the floor. I dared a peek inside the bowl, hoping not to suffer the visual trauma I had received from the last toilet.

Floating in the bowl was a small plastic tube. It was about an inch long, the width of a pencil, and closed at one end and open at the other. If there had been a cap, it was gone. The tube moved in a slow, circular motion around the bowl, hinting that the bowl had recently been flushed. Someone had tried to flush this thing, but its buoyancy had made it float back up into the bowl.

My exploration of the mysteries of the men's room at an exclusive country club was rudely cut short by that young man bursting through the door again. He had finally figured out that this was, indeed, the loo he had been looking for.

"Oh my God!" he shouted. This time he wasn't staring at me. He had noticed the body behind me.

"I didn't do it," I said.

He gaped at me, and I knew I had said the wrong thing. Never claim you didn't do something. People will immediately assume that you have.

Especially if you're in the wrong bathroom with a dead body.

I could practically hear the gears grinding in his head. "Sweet little old lady. Dead guy. Men's room." Every sacred taboo he had ever learned and every unseemly website he had ever visited rushed into his thoughts simultaneously. His young mind flashed with a dozen different interpretations of what had just occurred here, each more appalling than the last, and it froze him, actually froze him.

I took the opportunity to check the fourth and final stall. I saw nothing of note except some crude comments written on the wall.

Coming out of the stall, I gave the young man, who was still frozen, my sweetest sweet-little-old-lady smile.

"Gah!" he said, backpedaling out of the room. Not very eloquent, but I got the message clearly enough—don't smile at someone when they think you're a murderer. That smile would always be misinterpreted.

He was soon replaced by two bulky security men, who grabbed me and escorted me out of the bathroom. Another country club employee stood in the hallway, on his cell phone and talking to the police.

A large crowd of Cheerville's wealthy set stood

and stared. A couple of them took photos of me with their cell phones. Oh dear, I was about to go viral. I had never gone viral before. I'd avoided that sort of thing like the plague.

(It was good to keep a sense of humor in this sort of situation.)

Penny Price came up to us. "She didn't do it," she cried.

I had previously found her voice loud and grating, but now I was thankful for it. It meant that more of the gawpers would hear it. "We were standing in line for the ladies' room when a man came out of the men's room and said someone had been murdered. She went in after that to investigate."

A man appeared, looking pale and shaken and trailing a long tail of toilet paper out of the back of his pants.

"That was me," he said. "I was in one of the stalls. Someone was sitting in the next stall over. He got out, and a moment later, I heard a cry and a thud. I got finished as quickly as I could and came out. That's when I saw the body. The other person had already gone. He must be the murderer."

"We can't know that for sure," one of the security people said. "We'll have to hold this woman until the police come."

"Did anyone see a man leave the bathroom before this gentleman?" asked the young man who had discovered me. Now that I had a burly security officer holding each of my arms, he had defrosted.

Blank faces all around. I had to admit that I myself had been paying no attention to the men's room door until someone rushed out screaming bloody murder. That was the problem with witnesses to crimes. Nobody noticed anything until after the crime had been committed.

"What about security footage?" I asked.

"We don't have security cameras inside the building," one of the security men answered.

I turned to the man with the toilet paper tail. "Did you get a look at the man in the stall beside you?"

The man cocked his head. "What are you implying?"

I rolled my eyes, a habit I had picked up from my thirteen-year-old grandson. "Did he say anything? Did he have distinctive footwear?"

"Um, no. He did sound like he had a cold, though."

"He was sniffing?"

"Yeah, how did you know?"

"One of the stalls had a little plastic container floating in the bowl. It should still be there. That sort of container is often used to carry cocaine. It was next to a stall where someone forgot to flush."

That final comment made him flush, as in, his face, not the toilet.

"Oh. Sorry. I was … distracted."

"Fair enough," I said. "You should wash your hands, too, and get that toilet paper out of your pants."

The security people eased up on their grip but didn't let go. I had not entirely convinced them.

Mr. Toilet Paper Tail went off to get himself decent. A few minutes later, the police arrived.

In my brief time in this sleepy bedroom district, where the younger people mostly worked in the city and the older people mostly snoozed away their golden years doing not much of anything, I had gotten to know the Cheerville Police Department quite well. In fact, I had helped them on several cases.

That did not make me popular. The police didn't like to be one-upped by a woman in her seventies. The rank and file didn't know I used to be in the CIA. Perhaps that would have made them feel better. Perhaps not.

I was read my rights as Penny Price loudly objected. Then they escorted me from the building and drove me to the station. At least they didn't put me in cuffs.

That was right—I got arrested for investigating a crime. That was the level of professionalism of the Cheerville Police Department.

THREE

For the first time I could remember, Police Chief Arnold Grimal was happy to see me.

Happy to see me under arrest, that was.

He had heard over the police radio that I'd been arrested, and he stood at the front door of the police station with a big grin on his face and sweet-and-sour sauce on his chin. I'd interrupted him during one of his Chinese take-out meals. I did that a lot. It was an easy thing to do. The guy was supporting half of China with those takeouts.

"Well, well, well, Little Miss Perfect is in trouble with the law," he said.

I glared at him, but he wasn't fazed. He was enjoying himself too much.

"You know I didn't do it. I even have a witness."

"Oh, but we have a witness who puts you at the

crime scene. We need to hold you for questioning. If it turns out your story holds up, you'll be released." He said this all in a smug tone of voice. I could tell he knew I wasn't the murderer. I could also tell that he was going to enjoy every second of my humiliation.

And enjoy it he did. He stood there, rubbing his hands together with glee as I was fingerprinted and photographed. Then I was brought into an interrogation room.

"Don't I have the right to a phone call?" I asked as he sat down at the table opposite me. A policeman stood guard outside the door.

"Who do you want to call?" he asked.

"My former boss, perhaps." I didn't say "the head of the CIA," because this was being recorded. Only Grimal knew what I used to be.

He paled a little at that then rallied.

"You have the right to do so, of course," he said, "but I don't think you want to embarrass yourself in front of your boss by telling him you're under arrest."

"Falsely under arrest. It doesn't matter. I can handle this myself. Did your men recover that plastic container from the toilet bowl?"

"My men are professional law enforcement officers."

"Did they recover that plastic container from the toilet bowl?"

"Yes. But let's talk about you. What were you doing in the men's room?"

I recounted the events leading up to my entering the bathroom and all I had seen when I was in there. I also relayed to him what Mr. Toilet Paper Tail had told me.

"We've brought him in for questioning."

"I suppose you arrested him, did you?"

Grimal chuckled. "Of course not."

"Of course not. Can I go now?"

"Oh, I suppose. We'll sign the papers to have you released from custody. It might take a while. Red tape, you know."

This guy was going to get it. I didn't know how yet, but I was going to make him regret this little stunt.

The red tape took an hour. At last, I was released.

Octavian, the dear, was waiting for me in the front hall. After catching him up on what was going on, I had him drive me home.

"Do you think it was those mobsters?" He was referring to a gang that had a network of illegal casinos across the region. He had helped me break up that gang, not that he had volunteered for the job. The poor fellow had been kidnapped alongside yours truly.

"No, that gang is all broken up. The few who escaped the dragnet will be far, far from here. I don't know who this fellow was or why someone would stab him in the back while he was doing his business."

He kept one hand on the steering wheel and put the other on my own. "It must have been terrible to see that."

"I've seen a lot of death, Octavian. I've seen people blown apart by hand grenades. But yes, it was terrible. Death is always terrible."

The car went silent for a moment. We had both lost our spouses in nice, clean hospital rooms with plenty of family support around us. That had been terrible too.

He got me home, and I invited him in for some dinner. Neither of us had gotten the chance to eat. As Octavian sat on the couch, playing with Dande-lion—in other words, petting the little critter and enduring scratches all over his hands instead of further decreasing the value of his rented tuxedo—I made some pasta and heated up some tomato sauce. Hardly a five-hundred-dollar-a-plate dinner.

Octavian appreciated it, though. His stomach was grumbling by the time I served him. Mine was grumbling too. I opened a bottle of red wine for us to share.

"You all right?" he asked once we were about halfway through the meal. I hadn't spoken much.

"Oh yes."

"You're thinking about that case."

He didn't call it a murder. He called it a case. Octavian had figured me out pretty well.

"Yes, I am. Someone sat in the stall, waiting for him, perhaps sniffing cocaine. But how did he know the victim would go to the bathroom? And why murder him in such a public place? He was lucky he didn't get spotted."

Octavian thought for a moment. "It does seem strange. He was taking a huge risk, and yet at the same time, he did do a few things to cover his tracks, like hide in the stall. Maybe he felt he only had one chance to get this guy, or he had to kill him tonight for some reason. Who was the victim?"

"I don't know, but I intend to find out."

Early the next morning, I did.

I showed up at the police headquarters, where my good friend Arnold Grimal was hard at work at his desk.

Actually, he was looking at cute kitten photos on Facebook. Well, at least he wasn't eating Chinese takeout. I guessed they didn't deliver breakfast.

"I told the desk sergeant not to let you through," Grimal grumbled. A grumbling Grimal had become one of the mainstays of my life.

"I ignored him as usual," I said. "Cute kittens."

"Nothing wrong with taking a break," he snapped.

His entire career had been a break.

"Well, at least you're not looking at porn. Did you hear about that government official? He was just in the news. He obsessively looked at adult sites at work and managed to infect his entire department with malware."

Grimal nodded. "Kitten photos are safer. I read about that idiot. He accessed more than nine thousand websites. That's not a perversion, that's an addiction."

"It's funny how you can catch a virus for misbehaving online the same as you can in real life."

Grimal looked at me askance. Nothing made people more uncomfortable than old people talking about sex.

"Why are you here?" Grimal asked.

"You know why I'm here."

I sat. He stared. I remained seated.

"All right," he said with a sigh. "The victim's name is James Garfield, aged sixty-five."

"Garfield? As in the cartoon?"

"As in the president. He's a direct descendant. Or was. He was also president and chief archivist of the President Garfield Historical Association."

"I doubt that's why he got bumped off. What else did he do around town?"

"Nothing. He only moved here a week ago."

I cocked my head. "Really? He sure made enemies quickly."

"I was thinking that someone from his old town —he moved here from Cincinnati—might have followed him here, but the charity dinner organizers said all the guests were from the local area. Mostly Cheerville, Apple Bluff, and a few of the smaller towns."

"Surprising he even knew about the charity dinner," I said.

"One of the first things he did when he came to town was apply for membership in the country club. Someone told him about the dinner, and he bought a spot."

"A good spot? The tables were organized by how much you donated. I donated five hundred dollars and got stuck way at the back."

"He donated two thousand dollars and was right at the front."

"Well, he certainly must have made a splash."

I had a vision of him lying in two different

puddles next to the urinal and immediately regretted my choice of words.

"He was a retired property developer," Grimal said. "A major one. His net worth was well over five million dollars."

"People like that often make enemies."

"He obviously did. No obvious ones, though. We've only just started our investigation."

"Have you ruled out the kittens as suspects?"

"Har har."

"Did you send that plastic tube to the lab?"

Grimal nodded. "CSI is busy on all that. No fingerprints on the knife. Our perp wore gloves. There were fingerprints all over the stalls and bathroom door, so many that they obscure each other. It's going to be tough to get decent matches."

"That's too bad. Any other witnesses?"

"Just the guy in the next stall, a Mr. Geoffrey Pike. He said that the stall next to him was already taken when he entered and, um, sat down. He thinks the man had on gray slacks and brown shoes but couldn't be sure. Witnesses usually have bad memories of that sort of thing, and of course he wasn't paying much attention. The man in the stall next to him was sniffing, and Mr. Pike assumed he had a cold. Then he heard the man flush and leave the stall. After that, he heard Mr. Garfield cry out and fall to the floor. Mr. Pike called out, asking if he was all right, and when he didn't get an answer, he peeked under the stall and saw the body."

"And that's when he ran out into the hall, trailing toilet paper."

"Yes. And that's when you ran in and disturbed a crime scene. That's a criminal offense, you know."

I narrowed my eyes. Grimal looked away. He and I both knew he wouldn't press charges for that. That "arrest" the night before was just his way of getting back at me for making him look like a fool time and time again.

"Check on that plastic tube the murderer tried flushing down the toilet," I said. Well, *ordered*, really. "It probably contained cocaine or a similar substance."

"The lab is doing a chemical analysis. Initial report is that it's clean. The perp probably tried to flush it, and it floated back to the top. It might not have any residue left."

"Did James Garfield have any relations or friends in Cheerville or the surrounding area?"

"We're checking. None have come forward. No one at the country club knew of any."

"Why did he move here, then?"

Grimal shrugged. It was one of his more annoying gestures because he did it so often.

I stood. There was nothing more to find out here.

Finding a lead on a man who had moved to town only a week before and supposedly didn't know anybody was going to be tricky, but at least I knew one person who could help.

FOUR

My son was not what you would call a chip off the old block. He had never fired a gun, never been to a war zone, never traveled farther than England—where he got food poisoning from some fish and chips—and had certainly never overthrown a Third World dictatorship.

Needless to say, he never knew what my late husband, James, and I did for a living. He thought we worked in "international development" for the federal government, which was true as far as it went.

Frederick was a successful real estate agent and provided very well for his family. His wife, Alicia, was the brains of the family—sorry, Frederick—a particle physicist who worked with the CERN, the massive particle accelerator that had been responsible for so many important scientific discoveries I didn't understand. Their son, Martin, was thirteen and going through his early teen years fairly well—skateboarding, violent video games, shockingly messy room, occasional mood swings, decent grades, polite to his elders and kind to his juniors, avid reader. Not a bad balance.

They lived in a fine house with a white picket fence, in a little cul-de-sac in one of Cheerville's better neighborhoods. I pulled up for dinner early that evening. I had to question my son about poor James Garfield without his knowing that I was questioning him.

I knocked on the door. They had given me a key and said I could come in at any time, but I still knocked in order to give them their space. An important part of parenting was recognizing when your children had become adults with their own priorities and their own lives, and that had happened quite a while ago.

My son opened the door. "Hey, Mom, come on in."

Frederick went his own way not only careerwise but also physically. He had a few too many pounds, and his belly seemed to grow every year. That concerned me. I had gently nudged him in the direction of the gym, to no avail. Exercise was essential to health, although I had to admit I had gone too far in the other direction. All that combat training, somnambulant forced marches through jungle and desert, and hand-to-hand combat with thugs of a dozen nationalities had taken their toll. While at Frederick's age I had been at the peak of physical fitness, all the old injuries had come back to haunt me. Sometimes my ankles hurt. Sometimes my knees hurt. Sometimes everything hurt. I had recently joined a gym and was slowly trying to get myself back in shape. I had to take it easy, though. If I pushed it, I could end up worse than before.

We went into the living room, where my grandson, Martin, had his feet up on the coffee table, his hands on a controller, and his eyes glued to his Xbox.

"Hello, Martin," I said, tousling his hair before I forgot that he didn't like to be tousled anymore.

"Shhh," he said.

On the TV screen, Martin was transformed into a burly man in camouflage, crawling through the high grass of the African savanna. He had a sniper's rifle in his hand, easily identifiable as an M24 SWS, standard US Army issue. The graphics were quite realistic on games these days.

This was the quietest video game I had ever

seen him play. Insects buzzed, the sniper made a few soft sounds as he swished through the grass, and that was it.

Not quite. I heard the distant sound of conversation. Frederick had installed an excellent speaker system, and I could clearly hear the sounds were coming from the left. Martin moved in that direction.

"What's this game called?" I asked.

"Shhh. *One Shot, One Kill: Counterinsurgency Edition.*"

Sniper Martin crested a low rise, and a wide, dry riverbed came into view. Some men in black, their faces covered with kaffiyehs, were loading rocket-propelled grenades into the back of a Land Rover. A pit lay open at their feet, obviously where they had hidden the weapons until they could fetch them.

Hiding the weapons in a riverbed? What if it rained? These were either stupid terrorists or stupid game designers.

Martin switched to sniperscope view and scanned the scene. Through the crosshairs, we could see a man at the wheel of the Land Rover, half obscured by the tinted window. Three men were loading the weapons into the back of the vehicle.

"Check for sentries," I told him.

"Shhh."

"There's going to be someone—"

Bang! He took out one of the guys loading the weapons.

Bang! Bang! He got the other two.

The engine roared to life. Martin swiveled and fired, and the bullet pinged off the door, just an inch below the driver's-side window.

"Must be bulletproof," Frederick said.

Bang!

The screen went red then switched to an image of a terrorist rising out of the savanna grass to Martin's right, with an AK-47 and standing over Martin's dead body.

"Ugh! You guys distracted me!" Martin shouted.

"I told you to look for sentries," I said.

Martin did a classic teenage eye roll. "Why do you always pretend you know how to fight?"

I smiled, tousled his hair again just because I felt like it, and followed Frederick into the kitchen.

My daughter-in-law, Alicia, was in there making lasagna. Yes, a leading scientist who was a good homemaker too. She did it all. Better than I could. Although I had been at the top of my own and very different career, I was useless at cooking. The pasta

I had made for Octavian the night before was about as much as I could handle. Boil water, throw in spaghetti, wait until soft. Even that, I often messed up.

We chatted about nothing in particular for a time until my son gave me an in for what I really wanted to talk about.

"How was that charity dinner you went to with Octavian?" Frederick asked.

He still couldn't bring himself to say "boyfriend." He had lost his father only a few years before, so I didn't judge him. He'd met Octavian only once, and it had been awkward for them both.

I glanced into the living room to make sure Martin was still killing people, and I said in a low voice, "I didn't get to stay. There was a murder in the men's room."

"What?" Frederick and Alicia said in unison. Why did people always say that when they heard shocking news? They'd heard what I said, after all.

"A man named James Garfield."

My son's eyes grew wider. I was worried they might pop out and land on the floor. If one rolled under the refrigerator, we would never find it.

"James Garfield? I just met him a month ago. Tried to sell him a house."

"Tried to?"

Frederick's face grew hard. "Yeah, Chief Running Horse sold him a house instead. Stole my client."

Chief Running Horse was Frederick's main rival in the local real estate business. He ran Native Spirit Realty and made a killing. Chief Running Horse was no more Native American than I was Japanese. He was darker in skin tone, and he liked to pretend to be a Native American because it brought in business. Frederick couldn't stand him. Said he was a fraud, which of course he was. Frederick had even dug into his past and found proof that his real name was John Smith and he came from New Jersey. I suspected that was an alias. No one was really named John Smith.

Frederick had wanted to expose him but was afraid of a lawsuit that would damage his business as much as Chief Running Horse's.

"Did James Garfield buy an expensive house?" I asked.

"Yeah, that nineteenth-century brick place over on Blackberry Street. Sold for nine hundred fifty thousand dollars."

I let out a low whistle. No wonder Frederick was upset about missing out on that commission.

Our conversation got cut short when Martin slouched into the room.

"Done killing people?" I asked.

"Yeah. Hey, I'm reading a new series."

"What is it?" I asked.

"Zombots. It's about zombies who are robots."

"How can a zombie be a robot?"

He gave me a mischievous, childlike grin. "You'll just have to read it and find out. I'm already on book two, so you can borrow book one."

"I'd be happy to."

One of the most charming things about people his age was how they constantly switched from awkward adults into ebullient children. I felt grateful that I was present to see the last fading years of his childhood before the adult took over.

He ran off to his room. Something crashed in there. I could hear the sounds of objects being tossed aside as he burrowed through the travesty that was his bedroom floor before finding the book he sought. He returned a minute later, looking a bit flustered, and handed me a brightly colored paperback.

Zombots Book One: The Zomboroboticapocalypse.

"Bet you can't figure out how they became zombie robots," he said, jumping up and down.

"I'm still trying to figure out how to pronounce the title."

I looked at the cover. Several stiff-limbed people, their skin a greenish hue, had some sort of electronic gizmo stuck on the backs of their heads. They were chasing a group of plucky teens. There was always a group of plucky teens in these books.

"Hmm," I said, considering. "I can see why the series wasn't called Robot Zombies. Because that would mean that robots had died and come back to life as zombies. But these are zombie robots, zombies who have been turned into robots."

"Nope," Martin said in triumph. "They are regular people captured by a mad scientist and fitted with electrodes to turn them into zombies."

Young adult literature had changed a lot since the days of Nancy Drew and the Famous Five.

We ate our dinner in pleasant companionship. That was what I had moved to Cheerville for, to be with my son and my brilliant daughter-in-law and to watch my wonderful grandson grow up.

I had to admit, though, that this dinner was almost as unsettling as the one I had eaten with Octavian the previous night. My mind was still abuzz with questions about how poor James Garfield had been killed.

The first place to look for clues, of course,

would be his new house. I felt sure Grimal had sent his lackeys to check it out, and I felt equally sure that they had found nothing.

That, of course, was no guarantee that there was nothing to find.

It would be up to me, and all it would involve would be a little breaking and entering.

FIVE

Finding the house that James Garfield had bought was easy enough. Property sales were a matter of public record, so all I had to do was go to the Cheerville Records Office, fill out a form, and within fifteen minutes, I had the address—23 Blackberry Street.

I could have simply asked Frederick for the address, but I had no valid reason to do so. One of the chief rules of being a secret agent was to reveal as little about your intentions as possible. That had become so instinctive with me that I hadn't even considered asking my son.

I drove slowly down Blackberry Street, which, I supposed, at one time in the halcyon days when Cheerville was a sleepy little town and the city hadn't gotten so expensive that so many workers moved out to places like this, had been a little dirt lane where the locals collected blackberries. No more. Now it was lined with manicured lawns and two-story brick houses. Porsches and Jaguars were parked out front. The houses had garages, but why spend so much on a car and hide it in the garage?

Some of the houses were quite old, dating back to the time of the blackberries. These had a stylish charm that their newer neighbors tried and failed to emulate.

I passed by number 23. The curtains were drawn, and I saw no one.

After a second, slower pass, I decided it was safe enough and parked at the end of the lane.

One of the worst parts about getting older was that you became invisible. People discounted you, assumed you were harmless. Oftentimes, they didn't even see you. It was demoralizing to say the least.

At the moment, though, it was pretty darn handy.

I strolled up the street, admiring the fine houses, tidy lawns, and effusive flower beds. A woman walked past with her dog and said hello, her eyes unfocused. She would forget me within five minutes.

Once I got to number 23, I glanced around. A few doors down, a man washed his Mercedes with a soapy sponge. He faced me but was concentrating on his task. The dog walker was receding, her back to me. Now was a good time.

I walked up to the front door as if I belonged there, putting on my reading glasses as I did so. This would require some close-up work, and my eyes weren't what they used to be. The covered porch with its thick columns provided me a bit of cover as I slipped my lockpicks out of my pocket and jimmied the lock.

It sprang open without much fuss. An alarm in the front hall started beeping. I had thirty seconds to disable it.

I hurried over, as much as I could hurry these days, and pulled a code sheet out of my pocket. This was courtesy of a friend in the CIA. It included the override codes for every make and manufacturer of house alarms in the country. I checked the brand on the alarm, ran my finger down the list, and found it.

I punched in the code with seconds to spare. The light went from a flashing red to a steady green.

Every alarm had an override code for the use of technicians and law enforcement. It was illegal for me to have that list, but I had been in the CIA, not the Girl Scouts.

I closed the front door and got to work.

The interior was lovely, and I could see why it had sold for so much money. It had a fresh coat of paint that still lent a faint smell to the house. The wooden floors had been restored and polished, and there was an attractive oak banister up the curved stairway. I suspected it was original to the house.

James Garfield hadn't had much time to unpack. The living room, kitchen, upstairs bathroom, and master bedroom were the only rooms that had been fully fitted out. The second bedroom was filled with boxes, and the third bedroom was empty. The oak-paneled den, which I thought would make an excellent reading room, was half filled with boxes. Accessing the garage through a door in the laundry room, which had a brand-new washer and dryer still with their stickers on, I found the garage to be empty too. His car had been parked at the country club. No doubt it was in the impound lot by now. But I found no gardening equipment or anything else in there.

After making a quick initial pass, I started looking more carefully. The kitchen held nothing of interest, although I noticed there was no alcohol. I remembered his drinker's nose and ruddy cheeks and wondered about that. The boxes in the den contained books, mostly history and some quite old and probably rare. Apparently, he agreed with me that the den would make a good reading room, although he hadn't had time to buy bookshelves or even an armchair yet. The living room contained nothing but the furniture, all new.

I went upstairs. The master bedroom furniture was also all new. Had he kept his old house in Ohio? Was that why he hadn't moved the furniture to Cheerville?

Now that I was thinking of it, there weren't very many boxes. The boxes in the second bedroom contained clothes, some more books, a desktop computer, and various odds and ends. If he had unpacked everything, half of the house would have still been empty.

Yet according to the city records, he had purchased the house a month ago and taken possession a week ago, certainly enough time to get his things there from Cincinnati.

And he had certainly been slow about unpacking. He had a functioning router but hadn't unpacked his computer. I supposed he checked his email on a smartphone. It seemed odd that he hadn't unpacked his computer until I realized he didn't have a desk to put it on. And the walls were completely bare. No prints, no paintings or family photos. Nothing.

I got the impression that James Garfield was more interested in getting to Cheerville than living here. And yet he had spent almost a million dollars on a house.

The bathroom revealed no medications other than a common prescription for managing high blood pressure, not unusual for a man his age. There was also a prescription for Doxazosin. I didn't know what that was. With my phone, I took a photo of the bottle to look up later.

Now for the master bedroom, where people tended to keep their most personal possessions.

In a frame on the bedside table was the only photo in the whole house, and it was a curious one.

It showed a blond woman in her late twenties or early thirties, decked out in an expensive evening gown and wearing a diamond necklace and a sparkling ring. At least I thought they were diamonds. It was hard to tell because the photo had been taken from a distance and enlarged until it had become slightly pixelated. The woman was in profile and walking down a sidewalk. She did not appear to be aware that she was being photographed. At the edge of the shot was part of the person walking ahead of her, just the tail end of a dress, one foot, and part of a hand.

Had Garfield been spying on this girl? I took out my phone again and took a picture of it.

Just as I did, I heard the front door open.

Uh-oh.

What to do? There was almost no place to hide in this house!

A couple of footsteps sounded downstairs, so soft as to be all but inaudible. They stopped. Whoever it was hadn't passed much beyond the threshold. Was the newcomer wondering why the alarm hadn't started beeping? I hadn't reset it.

I tiptoed over to the closet, eased it open, and slipped inside amid a collection of expensive suits and dress shirts, closing the door except for a thin crack so I could see out.

The footsteps resumed, softly moving around downstairs. At times I couldn't hear them at all, and only the occasional creak of a floorboard told me the person was still moving. I opened my purse, where my trusty 9mm automatic was hidden. Good thing I still had my reading glasses on. I couldn't see the sights on my gun without them.

The footsteps stopped for a minute, replaced by the sound of boxes opening. Whoever it was had come here with a similar intention to my own.

The tread sounded heavy, as though it came from a man.

He began to ascend the steps.

Oh, great. If I got caught here by anyone with a legitimate reason to be in the house, I would get arrested for real this time.

The footsteps drew closer. He entered the bedroom.

Then he moved into view. Peeking through the narrow crack I had left in the closet door, I saw a tall man in buckskins, moccasins, and a feather headdress.

Chief Running Horse? What was he doing here? Real estate agents weren't supposed to go into a house after they had sold it, and they certainly shouldn't be rummaging through the boxes of the new resident.

He stood for a moment, looking around the room. Then he got on his hands and knees and looked under the bed. When he stood up again, I hoped he would walk out, but no, my luck just wasn't with me this week.

Instead, he opened the closet door.

"Aaaagh!" he shouted, leaping back at the sight of a little grandmother pointing a gun at him.

He stood there for a second, too stunned to speak. One of his feathers floated to the floor.

I didn't say anything at first either. What *did* one say in a situation like this?

While I had seen Chief Running Horse on lots of local commercials—his were even cheesier than Peter and Penny Price's—I had never met him. He had a broad face, skin that had seen more than one session in a tanning bed, straight black hair, and very pretty blue eyes. He was most definitely not Native American. Part Mexican or Italian, perhaps. I had seen Indians in old B Westerns who looked more convincing than him.

"What are you doing here?" he demanded at last. His hands were in the air. At least he didn't put one palm forward and say, "How?" I might have had to shoot him if he had done that.

"What are *you* doing here?" I asked.

"I'm selling this house. I'm a real estate agent. Haven't you seen me on TV?"

No one who was legitimately in a house and discovered an intruder felt the need to justify his presence.

"You already sold this house to James Garfield, who is now dead. You don't have any right to be here."

He paused for a second, fear in those bright-blue, very non-Indian eyes. "Did you kill him?" he asked.

"No, I'm investigating his murder."

"The police have already been here."

"The police are idiots."

Chief Running Horse nodded. As a professional con man, which was what anyone using a stolen identity to get ahead in their career certainly was, he would have already made quite an accurate assessment of the abilities of the local police.

"So what are you really doing here?" I asked, moving my pistol slightly forward to emphasize the fact that I wanted an honest answer.

"I was curious," he said. "No one knew James Garfield here, and then someone killed him. Plus, someone has been watching this house."

"Really? Who?"

He shook his head. His headdress looked quite impressive when he did that, but I was sure he already knew that.

"I don't know. The day after he moved in, I stopped by for a courtesy visit, and I noticed a black Mercedes parked across the street. I didn't think much of it. Then I drove by a couple of days later to check out another house in this neighborhood that might be going up for sale and saw the Mercedes again. Nobody parks on the street here. Visitors all park in the driveways, and there are no shops to go to."

I considered this.

"So you saw a suspicious car, and that was

enough for you to break into the house of a murdered man and rummage through his things? I don't buy it."

"I saw the person watching this house another time after that."

"When?"

"I was having a drink at the Candlelit Lounge late on the night of the murder. A couple of guys came in from the charity dinner, all shaken up and talking about how Garfield got killed. That's when I really got suspicious of the black Mercedes. I had noticed it before but didn't really think anything about it. Now I put two and two together. I figured that whoever owned that car might have bumped him off and might have wanted to get inside his house for some reason. So I drove over here. It was late, maybe eleven, and as I passed by, I saw a dark figure on the porch. Whoever it was spotted me and rushed around back. I was too scared to follow and drove away."

"What did this figure look like?"

"I don't know. It was dark, and I only saw him for a moment."

"Him?"

Chief Running Horse cocked his head and studied me. "I guess it could have been a woman. Can I put my hands down now?"

"No. Did you see the black Mercedes?"

"I didn't. The streets here wind all over the place. The driver could have parked on another street and cut across the yards. You don't want to park right outside a house you plan on breaking into."

Spoken like a career criminal.

"Did you call the police?"

"Um, no."

"Why not?"

"I was scared."

"Scared people call the police, especially after they've driven safely away. Here's what I think. I think you figured whoever killed James Garfield wanted to break into this house to steal something valuable. You came here with a spare key you shouldn't have in order to look for it."

"No, not at all!"

"Shut up. You're a fraud and most likely a criminal wherever it is you come from."

He put on a self-righteous look. "How dare you criticize my heritage!"

"Can it. You're not Native American."

His eyes narrowed. "You know what I think? I think you're not supposed to be here either. If you're on official police business, why did you hide in the closet? And where's your badge?"

I glared at him. He glared back at me, a far more impressive glare, considering he was the one with a gun trained on him.

I gestured with my gun toward the photo on the bedside table. "You know who that is?"

He turned and looked at it. From his expression, I could tell this was the first he'd noticed it.

"That's … creepy."

"Yes, it is. Recognize her?"

He shook his head again. "No."

"Tell me about James Garfield."

"The president? A terrible man. He broke many promises to my people."

"Don't make me shoot you. Tell me about James Garfield your client."

The fact that Chief Running Horse would mess with me when I had a gun on him told me a lot about him, none of it good.

"He contacted me a couple of months ago. He was in town for a visit, he said, staying at a B and B. He wanted to buy a house. First, he went to another real estate agent, Frederick Gold. But I stole Garfield right out from under that paleface's nose." He chuckled. "I showed him around various properties, and he picked this one. He liked it because it was old. A big history buff, that guy."

"Did he say why he wanted to move here?"

"He said he had relatives in town."

That was interesting. Grimal had said Garfield had no family here.

"What relatives?"

"He didn't say anything else about that. Garfield seemed like a pretty private person. You get a feel for people in my business. Some want to tell you their whole life story. Buying a house is a big step, and they see you as a new friend in a new phase of their life. Others just want a house and see you as just another salesman. He was more like that."

"Anything else you can tell me?" I wanted to wrap this up. I still had my gun leveled on him, and my arms were getting tired. His arms must have been getting tired too. They were still above his head.

"Not much. He bought the house right off. No mortgage. Said he had sold a lot of assets back in Cincinnati. Oh, he was in the business, too, but on the building side of it. Had a few contractors come through to check the place over and make sure it was a good investment."

"When's the last you saw him?"

"The night he moved in. I invited him to dinner at the Candlelit Lounge. It's my favorite place to eat, and I always take my clients there. They have good bison steaks. Bison is the meat of my people. Much leaner and richer in protein than the white man's industrial farm beef."

"Whatever. What did you talk about?"

"He had a lot of questions about Cheerville and high society here. I told him what I could, but I've always been given the cold shoulder by the rich in town. Bunch of racists."

"They may very well be," I said, remembering a collection of lawn jockeys I saw once at the Cheerville Seniors Center, "but I don't think they're judging you on your race."

He took on a sanctimonious look. "My people have always faced oppression."

"You mean criminals have always been put in jail for breaking the law. I suppose you're right. Can you remember anything unusual about the conversation? Did he ask any strange questions? Ask about anyone in particular? Did he seem nervous?"

"I could tell he was a recovering alcoholic."

"How so?"

"He had a drinker's face. The white man's fire-water had its grips on him. He didn't drink during dinner, but when I ordered a glass of wine, he stared at it. And stared and stared."

I gestured at the corner. "All right. You sit on

the floor over there, and I'm going to search this room. Then we'll move to the next room."

"I'll help you. We'll get this done faster if we split up."

"So that you can steal anything valuable? Not a chance. Sit."

He retrieved the feather that had dropped out of his headdress and sat. Meticulous fellow. Didn't want to leave any evidence of his being here. I rummaged through the boxes, keeping my gun within easy reach. He didn't try anything.

And I didn't find anything. Upstairs and downstairs, the boxes were filled with everyday household items and clothing. Nothing remarkable for a man of Garfield's age and wealth. The only unusual item was his book collection. I never realized there had been so many volumes written about a president who got assassinated less than seven months into his presidency. Besides the books, there were several volumes of clippings of old newspapers reporting the crime and the trial and execution of the assassin, Charles J. Guiteau.

After snooping through the final room, I turned to Chief Running Horse, who had obediently followed me around the house, sitting in a corner like a punished schoolchild.

"I don't understand this," I admitted.

"He's hiding something, and whatever it is won't be found in the stuff he brought from Ohio. Find out who that woman is in the photo, and you'll find out why he was murdered."

I nodded. "I think you're right. But I have another tough question—what am I going to do with you?"

SIX

He stood and gave me a smug smile. "You're going to let me go."

"You seem awfully confident," I said, pointing my gun at him.

He didn't bother putting up his hands. "You're breaking and entering just as much as I am. You can't call the cops, and you aren't going to shoot me. So it looks like you have no choice."

This man had the irritating habit of being right about too many things. I held out my hand. "Give me your key."

Without any hesitation, he reached into his fringed buckskin pants and pulled out the house key. I could tell he had expected me to ask him for it. After setting it on a box, he stepped away. "One thing I don't understand."

"Only one thing?" I replied. "You're better off than me."

"Why are you doing this? What's your angle?"

"My 'angle'? My angle is that I don't like seeing people get killed and murderers go free."

"Whatever. What are you getting out of it?"

This man just didn't understand. "A sense of justice. Some people actually want to improve the world."

He laughed as if I had said the stupidest thing he had ever heard. He obviously thought it was an excuse, that I was hiding something. Chief Running Horse or John Smith or whatever his real name was couldn't comprehend the idea that some people weren't one hundred percent selfish.

He held up his hand. "May the Great Spirit guide your path."

"Get out of here before I shoot you."

He chuckled and walked out the door.

I peeked outside from behind a curtain. Chief Running Horse strolled down the street and did not look back. Once he was gone, I checked that the coast was clear and got out of there.

An hour later, I was sitting in front of my computer with Dandelion curled up asleep in my lap and a cup of chamomile tea in my hand, searching the internet. Many people my age were helpless with computers, but I'd always kept up with any technology that might prove useful to my work, and the internet was so very useful.

At least when you weren't getting distracted by staring at cute kittens like the Cheerville chief of police was.

The first thing I looked up was Doxazosin. It turned out to be a medicine for managing enlarged prostate. Like the blood pressure medication, it was a common enough thing for a sixty-five-year-old man to take, and it gave me another insight into his murder.

Whoever killed him knew of his condition. An enlarged prostate put pressure on the bladder, forcing the patient to go to the bathroom more often. Some of my older male friends would run off two or three times during the course of a lunch. All the murderer had to do was wait in a stall, peeking out to check on each man who came in. Sooner or later, James Garfield would show up.

And Chief Running Horse had clued me in on another aspect of both James Garfield's character and perhaps his murder. Garfield was obviously a heavy drinker but was off the sauce. He was struggling, though, as was evidenced by his staring at the real estate agent's glass of wine.

I hadn't found any AA tokens or Twelve Step manuals in the house, and Grimal hadn't mentioned anything like that being found in his car or on his person. Garfield was going it alone. Sadly, I'd known a few drunks in my lifetime, and one coping mechanism they used was to have a lot of sweet drinks. This took care of the physical compulsion to always have a drink in hand, and the sugar from the drink gave a bit of a high similar to that from the sugar content in alcoholic drinks. I remembered finding a lot of fruit juice and soda in Garfield's refrigerator.

Of course, drinking a lot of anything would have made his trips to the bathroom even more frequent. Had the murderer known this about him too? That would have shortened the murderer's waiting time.

Next I uploaded the photo of that young woman to TinEye. This was a reverse image search engine that used image recognition software to find online matches. I was interested to see if he had gotten this image off the internet instead of taking it himself.

No luck. The search couldn't find anything even close. James Garfield was obviously taking pictures of this woman himself.

Obsession? Stalkers often raised their victims to an almost cult-like status. It would not be unusual for a stalker to frame a photo and put it by his bed.

I called Grimal. "Find the killer yet?" I asked.

"We will."

"Emphasis on the 'we.' A couple of questions. First, did you find anything to indicate that James Garfield was in a program for recovering alcoholics?"

"No. Judging from his face, he was a heavy drinker. Autopsy hasn't been done yet, though."

"Did you find his phone?"

"No. That's a bit odd, actually. It wasn't on his person or in his car, and no one turned in a lost phone at the country club."

That was too bad. It might have had more photos on it that could have given me a lead. Perhaps the killer took it. Did our knife-wielding, cocaine-sniffing bathroom loiterer know Garfield had been taking pictures of that woman?

"Do you have any women complaining about stalkers in town?"

"No. We had a case last year, and the judge gave the guy a restraining order. An ex-husband who couldn't deal with the woman getting a new love and moving on with her life. I had to arrest him for breaking it. He wasn't violent or anything, but he still got a big fine."

"It wasn't James Garfield?"

"No," Grimal said, sounding confused.

"What did the woman look like, the one who took out a restraining order?"

"Forties. Heavyset. Short brown hair. Why?"

"Never mind." I hung up.

I petted Dandelion and considered all this. It looked like I was at a bit of a dead end. Whenever that happened in a case, I realized that I needed to take it from a different angle. Garfield's possessions and physical state had given me all the clues they were going to, and now I needed to go down a different path if I wanted to learn more.

But what path? I didn't know, so I did what everyone did to waste time these days—I browsed the internet.

James Garfield had a pretty big online footprint. As Grimal had said, he had been a major player in Ohio's real estate development, buying land and building on it. He had made millions and had owned a sizeable company.

Then suddenly, earlier this year, something had changed. The *Cincinnati Enquirer* reported that he had announced his retirement and had sold his business. The paper expressed surprise at this move since it had been so sudden and his business had been growing. Another article from a history magazine reported that Garfield had recently donated $500,000 to the James Garfield Presidential Library.

There was also the website of the James Garfield Historical Society with some articles by the man himself. It was all very specialized and technical. I wondered how many readers these articles got. I also found him referenced in JSTOR, an online archive of academic articles. It was a subscription-based service, so I couldn't read beyond the abstracts. Those were enough to tell me he had written several lengthy articles about the Garfield presidency for leading historical journals. The murder victim had been quite the accomplished historian.

Digging deeper into the news reports and going back several years, I found many articles about his business successes. What I didn't find was any mention of family or his personal life. Garfield had either been a very private man or didn't have any family and personal life to speak of. I was beginning to suspect the latter.

"So short of going to Cincinnati, how am I going to find anyone to tell me about this fellow?" I asked Dandelion. All she did was stare at me for a moment then start licking herself. Not a terribly helpful answer.

I shooed her off and decided to go to the one place I knew Garfield had visited—the Cheerville Country Club.

After driving up that long, sweeping driveway and having a uniformed attendant park my humble little Nissan next to all those Mercedes and Jaguars, I was ushered inside to the membership office.

The gentleman behind the desk greeted me with a handshake and smile that lacked warmth. I realized I had not sufficiently dressed for the part. Not so long ago, I wouldn't have even been able to enter his office. Women had not been admitted to most country clubs even as recently as the '90s. They still weren't welcome in most.

I chatted with him amiably enough about how I was interested in making some social connections. He asked me about my work, and I spun him the usual tale that I had spun all my professional life, then he gave me what I really wanted—the tour. I needed to see more of this building and figure out the layout and setting of the murder.

"Allow me to show you our facilities," he said with a faint hint of weariness and disparagement. I suspected he had spent some time in England. No one could be as simultaneously rude and polite as the English.

First, he showed me the function hall where we'd had the charity dinner. It seemed cavernous and a bit spooky now that it was empty of people. The tables were still in place, and I realized that the murderer would have wanted one of the cheaper tables near the back. He seemed to know his target well, so he would have wanted to sit near the back to watch Garfield drink and gauge the time when he would get up and go to the john. The murderer wouldn't have wanted to sit in the bathroom stall for too long; his absence might have been noted. I imagined him waiting, watching, perhaps not too far from me and Octavian, counting how long Garfield could hold it.

As we turned to walk back out, I noticed beside the big double doors the stand for the maître d'. I remembered him taking our names and looking in a leather ledger before having a waiter seat us. That ledger still sat on top of the stand.

It would have the names of every guest at the charity dinner. It would have the name of the murderer. I needed to get that ledger.

The membership officer steered me out into a hallway and through a lounge. Men sat in small circles, smoking and chatting. State law forbade smoking in such places, but this was an esteemed country club. They did what they wanted.

Waving my hand in front of my face to clear the air, I listened as the membership officer droned on about all the advantages of the club. He did not mention the advantage of getting lung cancer.

Just as we were turning to leave and hopefully go to a room with a higher oxygen content, a waiter stopped in front of us and let out a shriek.

"It's the murderer!"

I recognized the young man who had first discovered me in the men's room. "I am not a murderer, young man," I told him.

He sputtered. "I mean, it's the woman who went into the men's room!"

Everyone was now staring at us, of course. This was just what I needed.

"Albert, get ahold of yourself!" the membership officer barked.

"Sorry, sir," Albert said. He turned to me. "Sorry, ma'am. I didn't mean to imply you stabbed that guy. It's just that, I mean, you were almost standing in a puddle of his—"

"Albert!" the membership officer barked again.

"Um, sorry." Albert made himself scarce.

We left the lounge as quickly as possible, followed by the gaze of a dozen smoking rich men.

"Sorry about that," the membership officer said. "We're all a bit distraught over what happened the other night. You were the woman who rushed to investigate?"

I tensed. Did I note a hint of suspicion in his question? I had hoped not to be recognized, and now Albert the Hysterical Waiter had announced to everyone who I was.

"Yes, I was standing in line for the ladies' room when someone rushed out saying a man had been killed. I rushed in to see if I could help."

"It must have been quite traumatizing."

"More for him than me."

He gave me an odd look. Gallows humor was common in the field as a coping mechanism. Sometimes I had to remind myself that civilians didn't do that.

The membership officer seemed to rush through the rest of the tour, obviously wanting to get rid of me. He showed me the terrace, the café, the library, the private meeting halls, the gardens, and even the golf course. I would have rather skipped the golf course, but I wanted to see the layout of the place and figure out how best to break in.

I needed that ledger from the maître d'. The fact that it was still sitting there two nights after the charity dinner told me that it was rarely if ever moved. All I needed to do was break in, photograph the guest list from that evening, and get out without being spotted.

Simple enough for a woman of my talents.

If only.

SEVEN

I stifled a yawn. Night work had once been a walk in the park for me, but as I got older, I found I tired more easily.

The country club didn't have the best security. Only one rotund, unarmed officer patrolled at night, zipping around the grounds in a golf cart, of all things. The locks on the doors, I had noticed on my tour, were cheap and easily picked.

On the other hand, the cameras were well placed, covering all approaches. The terrain was what really kept it secure. There was open ground all around, and while the lighting was dim and the property was far enough from the road that the only person I had to worry about spotting me was the aforementioned rotund watchman, there was no way for me to get to a door without being filmed.

That wasn't such a big deal. My handy disguise kit had turned me into a rotund man not unlike Mr. Golf Cart. I had added a paunch and a short blond beard, wrapped a scarf tightly around my chest to hide my most womanly trait, and hidden my hair under a black cap. The cameras would see a short, fat man of indeterminate age, not a short woman of a certain age.

Having cased the building, I decided my best option was to come at it from the side, through a stretch of woods that was half on, half off the property. I was relieved to see that there was no fence, otherwise I would have had to repeat the embarrassment of trying to cut through the chain links with hands that had lost too much of their strength. That had happened a couple of missions ago and had been a blow to my self-esteem. It didn't help that I had been breaking into a nudist colony.

But that was another story.

I got to the edge of the woods and looked out over the broad expanse of lawn between me and the side of the building. It would take a good two or three minutes to cross that stretch of open ground.

I waited. In the distance, I heard the electric whine of the golf cart. It grew louder, and soon, it whizzed around the corner of the building. I could see the little security man inside. He picked up speed and straightened out. Heading straight for me.

I ducked behind a tree. After another few seconds, he made a sharp turn and rose up on two wheels.

"Yee-haaaw!" he shouted into the night air.

He landed on all four wheels again and zipped off toward the backyard, where the garden and the golf course lay.

Now was the time to move. If he were driving through the golf course, he would be back there awhile.

I hurried, as fast as I could hurry these days, across the open stretch of lawn.

"Yee-haaaw!" I heard faintly from behind the building. He sounded distant. Good.

I glanced around as I moved to the building, seeing no one. Of course, the cameras could see me, but I had noted the name of the security company that had installed them during my tour of the country club, and I knew it was one that didn't offer real-time monitoring services. Instead, these were cameras meant to deter break-ins and find any culprits after the fact. In reality, they were cameras meant to lower the club's insurance premiums. This was a common practice. If you could convince the insurance company you had a "security system" and "security guards," you got a much lower rate, even if the quality of those protections was pretty low, as was the case here.

The quality of the locks was low too. I got through in less than a minute.

The interior was pitch black, the curtains drawn to the feeble light outside. I switched on a mini Maglite and found I stood in a small meeting room.

I moved quickly to the door, wanting to get to an interior room without windows just in case the golf cart stunt driver came past again. It wouldn't do to see a light shining in the window.

I entered a second room that led me to the main hall. Here, I switched off my light. I knew the way now, and the exit signs had little red lights on them that gave me just enough light to see.

Within a matter of minutes, I was at the maître d's stand, had found the right section in his book, and was using my phone to take photos of the relevant pages. Technology could be a wonderful thing. Back when I was still doing this sort of sneaking around for a living, I would have had to write down the names or steal the logbook, neither a desirable option. Of course, I could have always used one of those miniature cameras the government issued us, but then I would have had to develop the film myself. I never could stand the smell of those chemicals. Made me sneeze.

Which was what I did as I finished taking a photo of the last page.

Come now, Barbara, where is your professionalism? Back in the day, that could have gotten you killed!

I sneezed again. What was doing that?

A strange smell tickled my nostrils. It took me a minute to detect what it was—marijuana.

"Bob, is that you?" called a sleepy male voice. Sleepy or stoned.

The voice had come from around the corner of the main hallway. The maître d's stand stood in front of the double doors to the function room, now closed. The main hall ran to the right and left before turning. One direction went to the infamous men's room. The other led to that smoky lounge. It was from there that the voice came.

"Bob?" the man called again. It sounded closer this time.

I turned off my phone and hid behind the stand. There was no other cover.

Another wave of marijuana smoke reached me. I held my nose to resist sneezing again.

"Bob! Dude, why don't you answer?"

I gave a quick peek out from behind the stand

and saw a figure come around the corner, looking sinister and dark in the dim light of the hallway.

Well, not really sinister. Sinister people didn't generally say "dude."

The footsteps approached. I peeked again. The figure passed under the red light of an exit sign. That was enough for me to recognize him.

It was Albert, the waiter who'd discovered me in the bathroom and later called me out in the lounge, making me look ridiculous in front of all those rich cigarette smokers.

He shuffled along, eyes hooded, a joint in his hand. He held it to his lips and took another toke. I ducked back behind the stand as he drew closer.

Albert let out a rush of air, filling the hallway with a pungent stench.

I let out a sneeze powerful enough to shake the rafters, if there had been any.

"Bob? What are you doing, man?"

The waiter came around to the back of the stand. I shined a light in his face and pointed my gun at him.

"Dude, stop messing around," he said, shielding his bloodshot eyes from the glare. He blinked for a minute to adjust them then saw who held the flashlight and what she held in the other hand.

"Aaagh! Ugh! Aaagh! Baaaah!"

It wasn't exactly Shakespeare, but I think it reflected his feelings quite accurately.

"Shut up," I snapped.

He shut up.

I got to my feet, trying to look menacing. The effect was somewhat ruined by me having to lean on the stand and both my knees making loud popping sounds. Just what was popping inside there, anyway?

"Wh-what are you doing here?" he said, shaking all over. Oh dear, I thought the pot had made him paranoid. Or maybe coming up against someone in the dark with a gun did that. I didn't know much about drugs except how to take down drug cartels.

"What are *you* doing here?" I countered.

"I work here!"

"In the middle of the night, with the lights off?" I sneezed. "Put that thing out!"

He stubbed it out on the side of the maître d's stand, leaving a little black burn mark. I waved my hand in front of my face to clear the air.

"I'm, like, the night watchman," he said, still trembling.

"No you're not. The night watchman is racing around the grounds in a golf cart. Is that the Bob you were calling out to?" I needed to know how many idiots I was dealing with here.

"Yeah, that's Bob."

"Anyone else here?"

"You."

There was a reason they called it dope.

"Anyone else *besides* me?"

"Are you alone?"

"Yes."

"Then no."

I resisted the urge to smack him.

He peered at my face. My voice did not match my disguise.

"Wait a minute, you're that old chick from the bathroom."

"That old chick has a gun trained on you. Mind your manners."

"Uh …"

"The proper response is 'sorry.'"

"Sorry."

"So why are you here killing brain cells alone in the dark?"

"I live here."

"If this place hired a full-time residential staff member, I seriously doubt it would be you."

"No, like, they don't know. Except Bob. He's cool. I sell him weed. My parents kicked me out of their house, and I don't have anywhere to live, so I sleep on a sofa in the lounge. I take my showers in the golf club changing room. I've been doing it, like, for months, and nobody has noticed."

He smiled at that then broke into giggles. I waited for him to finish. It took a while. He was quite the giggler.

"Okay, Albert, here's the deal. I'm investigating the murder of James Garfield, the guy who was stabbed in your men's room. Another country club member did it. That member attended the charity dinner, so I snuck in here to take pictures of the guest list to narrow down the suspects. Now I'm going to leave. You will tell no one that you saw me, and I'll tell no one that you're a drug dealer sleeping on the couch at your place of work. You get to keep your job and your liberty, and I get to get rid of you."

"Uh, okay."

Well, that was easy. It looked like he still had a few brain cells after all. I turned to leave.

"Wait!" he called after me.

I turned around. "What?"

"I think I saw the murderer."

EIGHT

I studied him. Albert was not what you would call a reliable witness. "Tell me more," I said.

"You said the victim's name was James Garfield?"

"Yes."

"That, like, rings a bell. A guy at the dinner pointed him out to me and told me to give him a free glass of wine on him but not to say who it was from."

The murderer wanted to get Garfield drunk. That certainly would have made him an easier target.

"What happened?" I asked.

"Uh, let's see …" His voice trailed off.

"Wake up. Try to see through the fog you put in your brain. This is important."

He stared at me blankly for a moment, his eyes almost shut, then they opened a little as a couple of sleepy synapses fired.

"Oh yeah! So I, like, went over there with a bottle of red and a bottle of white. People have their preferences. Personally, I don't like alcohol. It's, like, unhealthy."

"You've hardly chosen an improvement. Go on."

"So I go up to him, saying an anonymous friend wants to offer him a free glass of wine, and he just stares at me. Like really stares at me for, like, a full minute. Like it was weird."

"And, like, what happened next?" Oh dear, now he had me doing it.

"Well, actually, he wasn't staring at me. He was, like, staring at the bottles. Staring at the bottles like you would stare at a hot woman. Well, not you. Unless you're a, I mean, like, I wouldn't want to assume—"

"Go *on*." I was losing patience. Actually, I had lost it about ten seconds into this conversation, but now I was fantasizing about shooting him.

"Then he sort of, like, shudders and looks away. He said he didn't want any."

"Anything else?"

"Yeah, when I came back to give him the large orange juice he ordered, instead he asked me who offered him the wine. I said the guy wanted to remain anonymous. He kept pressing me and pressing me to answer, and I had to make an excuse to get out of there."

"What can you remember about the man who offered Garfield the wine?"

"Um, he was sitting near the back. Near the door."

I smiled. That was what I'd thought.

"What did he look like? Was he with anyone?"

"Um, I can't remember if he was with anyone. He was, like, maybe in his fifties. Pretty fit. Still had his hair, although it was, like, going gray."

"Anything else?"

"He gave me a ten-dollar tip. I sure remember that. Let me think … uh … no. I can't think of anything else."

"Give me your phone number."

"Why?"

"I want to question you once you've sobered up. Don't smoke any more tonight and don't smoke tomorrow. I'll call you then."

"You're not going to tell on me, are you?"

"Not if you behave."

"So if you're a cop, why are you, like, sneaking around?"

"Because I'm not a cop, at least not in the way you think. I just like to see justice done, and the cops in Cheerville are useless."

He laughed. "Dude, they so are! Like, I was smoking with Brad and Chad and Chad's dad in the park and—"

"I don't care," I said. It appeared every criminal in town knew that the Cheerville Police Department was useless. Maybe that was why there was such a high murder rate.

After a final warning to Albert to stay sober, and after confiscating his joint, I headed back the way I came. I got to watch Bob do wheelies on the golf cart before disappearing out of sight, then I did a disappearing act of my own.

I settled in at home for a good night's sleep. The murderer obviously knew Garfield well and had even tried to get him off the wagon. That was a cruel thing to do to someone trying to kick alcoholism, but considering he planned to plant a knife in Garfield's back, I guessed he was beyond being nice to the poor guy.

The odd thing was, Garfield apparently didn't know him at all. The murderer could sit in the same room as his intended victim without fear of being spotted.

The next morning, I called Grimal. The desk sergeant tried to fob me off with some story of Grimal being busy. I knew better. Grimal was almost never busy.

Once I got him on the line, I grilled him about what progress he had made.

I was not surprised to find out that he hadn't made much headway.

"The lab reports came back," he said. "That plastic capsule we fished out of the toilet had no traces of anything. Whatever it contained, getting flushed cleaned it out. The coroner found out some interesting things about Garfield. Serious liver damage due to long-term heavy drinking. No trace of alcohol in the blood, though."

"From what I've learned, he was trying to kick the habit."

"He must have started that recently. The coroner said his liver was bad. He explained that it starts to heal itself pretty quickly after you quit the booze. Within a few weeks. That hadn't happened, though."

"Does that work for kicking a serious Chinese takeout habit?"

"Very funny. My fortune cookie today said I'd have some luck this week. Maybe you'll decide to move away."

"More likely, I'll solve the murder for you. Did the coroner say anything else?"

"Yes, the murderer was left-handed and pretty strong. One determined stab straight into the body. This guy had no hesitation, no scruples."

Albert had described a fit man in his fifties. A bit of cocaine would have added to his strength.

"What else do you think the plastic container could have had?" I asked.

"Cocaine is the most likely answer," Grimal said. "Cheerville has all the usual types of drugs, but for the upper class, it's most likely cocaine."

"Arrest any dealers lately?"

"No."

Of course not. "Do you have anything else to tell me?"

"No."

Of course not. I felt pretty lonely when I had to solve murders in this town.

I hung up. Next I called Albert, my dope-smoking waiter friend.

It took several calls before he picked up.

"It's about time," I said.

"Who is this? Your number isn't appearing."

"That's because I have it shielded. This is the nice old lady you met in the men's room."

"Oh God."

"Not God, young man, but I have equal authority over you. Are you sober?"

"I'm at work."

"That doesn't answer my question."

"Yes, I'm sober," he said with the same tone my grandson used when I asked him if he'd done his homework.

"Where are you now?"

"In the kitchen. I'm moving to the back hall so no one can hear us."

"Yes, I suspect you're accustomed to clandestine phone calls. Can you remember anything more about the man who sent James Garfield the free drink?"

"Uh, no."

"You never saw him before?"

"Not that I can remember."

"You never sold him cocaine?"

"I don't do that!"

"Oh yes, you only sell marijuana. You're such an angel. Was the man left-handed or right-handed?"

"How am I supposed to remember that?"

"Did you notice what kind of car he drove?"

"I don't work parking the cars, only inside serving members."

"Very well. Do you know who in the club drives a black Mercedes?"

"Tons of people."

"Hmm, I suppose you're right. What about photos of members? Is there some sort of collection of pictures? For the golf players or member of the month or something like that?"

"Uh, no. Sometimes members end up in the paper. Most are bigwigs in town, so they get into the papers sometimes."

"Aha! Now we're getting somewhere. Once you get off work, I want you to do a search through articles on the *Cheerville Gazette* website. Search for news about members and look at the pictures for that man who wanted to buy Garfield a drink. Oh, and try to sneak a peek at the membership records and see if any members besides Garfield moved here from Ohio."

"I have things to do," he moaned.

"Like smoke dope and eat too many Doritos? You have more important things to do than that, like helping me solve a murder. Now get to it. I'll call you later this evening to check on your progress." I hung up before he could make another objection.

Now what to do?

I brewed myself a tea and thought things over. I was at a bit of a dead end. Albert had given me some vital clues, but I had to rely on his initiative to move the case forward. Hardly an ideal situation.

Besides, even if he did match the man who sent the drink to Garfield with an identifiable member of the country club, Albert would make a terrible witness. Any halfway-decent defense attorney would be able to rip his testimony apart.

I needed more solid proof. The problem was, I had no idea how to find it.

As usual when I got stuck on a mission, opportunity opened up along another avenue, one I hadn't anticipated—Octavian called.

"Hello, pretty lady!"

The sound of his voice always cheered me up.

"How are you today?" I asked, going from pensive and worried to bright and chipper in one second.

"Just fine. Guess what? You're talking to the newest member of the Cheerville Country Club."

"Why? You said you couldn't stand the people."

"I can't, but you need help with your case. You got caught in that bathroom, so everyone there will be on the lookout for you. Who knows? The murderer might even know about you. Nobody will suspect me, though. I can be your eyes and ears. The Dynamic Duo fighting crime. Like Batman and Robin, or the Green Hornet and Kato, or Bert and Ernie."

"Bert and Ernie fought crime?"

"Probably. And if they did, I'm sure they could bust this case wide open."

"Which one of us is Bert?"

"I don't know. Why does it matter?"

"Because Bert is yellow and grumpy. I don't want to be yellow and grumpy."

"Don't take this literally. It's a metaphor."

"Simile."

"Pardon?"

"It's a simile. A simile is a comparison that uses 'like' or 'as.' A metaphor doesn't."

"What did you do in the CIA, teach English?"

"No, but we learned to be precise. I really don't want you getting into this, Octavian. It's too dangerous, and you lack the training."

"What's the danger? I'm going to be hanging out in a country club, for Pete's sake!"

"With a man who sticks silver steak knives into the backs of people he doesn't like. This is a bad idea, Octavian."

"I'll be careful. Even more, I'll be useful. I

thought up a neat trick in that miniature submarine, didn't I?"

I was about to object again, but the words died in my throat because I suddenly saw where he was coming from. It was the same place I had come from when I rushed to solve the first murder I came across after my retirement. You couldn't infiltrate bases and get in gunfights for a living and just give it all up to do needlepoint and watch daytime television. For a while, I was bored stiff and completely directionless for the first time in my adult life. Having a member of my book club get murdered was like a gift from heaven.

Then I started digging under the skin of this inconspicuous little town. What I found shocked me —murders, deadly rivalries, organized crimes, weird subcultures. It delighted me too.

Octavian was feeling the same boredom, the same lack of direction. He had been a star in the business field. While that wasn't as dangerous as my career, it was just as demanding. You couldn't switch from that to seniors yoga without feeling a sense of loss.

Octavian craved some excitement in his life, and I knew him well enough to know that he wouldn't stop investigating just because I asked him to.

He was too much like me.

"Oh, all right," I conceded. "Just be careful, okay? Oh, and the murderer is left-handed and might drive a black Mercedes. Keep an eye out for a healthy man in his fifties with graying hair."

"All right. How do you know all that?"

"A stoner, a Chinese takeout addict, and a fake Native American told me."

He laughed, not because he disbelieved me but because the whole thing excited him.

"You're a thrill a minute, Barbara. Talk to you soon."

He hung up. While I had been talking with him, another idea popped into my head.

If I were a rabid history buff who had just moved to a town that was founded before the American Revolution, where would I visit?

I headed to the Cheerville Historical Society.

The historical society was located just on the edge of the town square in a little one-room schoolhouse built in the early nineteenth century. It was an attractive structure made of stone, but I always thought it was rather small for a historical society. Not that I had ever been inside. No one I knew had ever mentioned visiting either.

I parked and walked across the village green, remembering how just a few weeks before, I had been given a supporting role in a major motion picture called *Freedom's Hero: The Fight for America*, a historical action picture about the American Revolution. My smile at the memory of being in a movie with Cliff Armstrong, Hollywood's greatest male star, dimmed as I approached the schoolhouse. Someone had tried to murder Cliff Armstrong as he did a scene while coming out of that schoolhouse and had nearly killed the entire crowd, my grandson included. It was remarkable how many seemingly lovely spots had been the site of tragedy and madness.

The heavy wooden door to the schoolhouse had a little sign stating "Cheerville Historical Society, established 1897." That made it quite an old historical society, I supposed.

I entered, and a little bell above the door jingled. Inside, the schoolhouse was preserved as it would have been 150 years ago.

Well, almost.

A row of scarred wooden desks complete with inkwells and slate boards stood in three rows facing a blackboard. A few old maps adorned the walls, showing the British Empire owning much of the globe and the French owning much of the rest of it. My, how times had changed. The back wall had a few displays about the history of Cheerville and some shelves of modern books and a microfilm reader.

In a corner at a desk sat a middle-aged woman dressed as a nineteenth-century schoolmarm, or at least the stereotypical severe, humorless school-marm of every old movie. She wore a starched black dress with a high collar that looked unneces-sarily uncomfortable. She had that frown the old movies and paintings always gave schoolmarms too.

The smartphone in her hand sort of ruined the effect.

She was playing a video game, which blooped and bleeped and blarped as she frantically tapped away.

"Hello," I said when she didn't look up.

Bloop, bleep, bloopity-bloop, blarp.

"Hello," I repeated, louder this time.

She glanced up, fingers still dancing across the screen.

"One second," she said breathlessly.

Blarp. Bloop. Bloopbloopbloop, blarpity-boop.

"Yesssss!" She pumped her fist in the air. Some-how, I didn't picture nineteenth-century school-marms being much on fist-pumping.

She put down her phone. "Made it to level ten. How can I help you?"

"I'm new to town, and I was curious to see what you had here."

She stared at me. When no words were forth-coming, I added, "I'm interested in history. I feel that if I'm going to spend my golden years here, I should know something about the history of Cheerville."

"Are you a schoolteacher planning a trip for your class?"

"No."

"Are you an academic writing a book?"

"No."

"You're not with the state inspection board, are you?"

"Um, no."

"So why are you here?"

She stared at me with open suspicion. I blinked. Had I said something wrong?

"I'm here because I'm new in town, and I'd like to learn some local history," I repeated.

"That's odd," she muttered, glancing at her phone. She looked back at me. "So what would you like to know?"

I shrugged. "I'm not sure, since I don't know much about the history of the area."

She let out a weary sigh. Obviously, she wanted to get back to her game and was not happy with this unexpected, and unwelcome, interruption. She pushed a sign-in book and a pen across the desk to me.

When I looked at the page, I saw why my appearance had struck her as so unusual. The last person to visit had done so a week ago.

Then I noticed who it was.

James Garfield.

NINE

James Garfield had signed in early one morning exactly a week before. There was a column listing the time when each visitor came in and when they left. He had stayed nearly three hours. I filed the time and date away in my memory. It was the only secure confirmation of his whereabouts for any time before the murder.

Garfield had a distinctive signature, very elaborate and old-fashioned. It looked familiar, and after a moment, I realized he had imitated the president's signature.

When looking up President Garfield, I had noticed that all the history pages on presidents included their signature, just in case you came across one in a rummage sale or something. The murder victim had taken his hobby one step beyond to outright imitation.

Pity he got assassinated just like his namesake.

The schoolmarm gestured to the bookshelf. "There are some local history books over there. The microfilm machine has all the old issues of the *Cheerville Gazette*."

"Aren't those all on their web page?"

She looked at me like I had just passed wind.

"The *Cheerville Gazette* was founded in 1827. The online back issues only go back to 1998."

"I see," I said, somewhat abashed. Historical research had never been my forte.

It still wasn't. I went over to the bookshelf and rummaged through the books. The schoolmarm went back to her game.

Bloop. Bleep. Bleepity-bloop. Blarp-bloop.

I found several books on the early colonial days, the little battle that had happened on our village green during the American Revolution, and books on Cheerville's more recent history. There was even a book on the history of the Cheerville Historical Society. A history of people studying history? I would have to keep that one in mind in case I ever suffered from insomnia.

One slim volume was titled *Presidents in Cheerville*. I flipped through it. Almost half of the text was taken up by the story of a brief visit George Washington had made to the town. He had been passing through and prayed at our lovely old church. Then he left. He couldn't have been in Cheerville for more than two hours, but the book managed to draw that out to thirty pages of description. Apparently, not much happened in Cheerville back then either.

A few other presidents had stopped by. Grover Cleveland had even stayed the night. But the most important chapter was the one on James Garfield.

I felt a little prickle in my neck, knowing that the victim had held this very same book almost exactly a week before.

The bleeping and blooping had stopped.

I turned. The schoolmarm was staring at me.

"Find what you need?" she asked.

"Yes."

She went back to bleeping and blooping.

I read the chapter. In 1868, Garfield, who was not yet president but was already a prominent congressman, had passed through town and stopped at the town square to give a speech in support of the gold standard and against those newfangled greenbacks, which weren't backed by anything. It was hard for people in the age of debt and credit to understand, the book explained, but in the nineteenth century, consumers didn't trust money that wasn't either made of precious metal or backed by precious metal. The issuance of paper currency had blossomed in the United States during the American Civil War as a stopgap measure to bolster the economy. After the war finished, the government moved to make paper currency permanent and get rid of the gold standard. Garfield had been against that because he said that path "would lead this nation to a ruination of debt and speculation."

I rummaged through the rest of the materials for a time and found nothing else of interest.

I headed for the door. The bleeping and blooping stopped again.

"You haven't signed out," the schoolmarm said.

I turned. "Excuse me?"

She pointed at the ledger. "Every visitor must put the time they entered and the time they leave."

I had visions of her picking up a ruler, smacking my wrist, and making me sit in the corner, wearing a dunce cap.

She certainly looked like she wanted to do just that.

I dutifully signed out and, just to be irritating, wasted a couple of more minutes inside the schoolhouse, looking at the displays. As I left, I saw her correcting my departure time.

That had me chuckling all the way across the village green.

As I got into my car, my phone rang. It was Grimal.

That surprised me. The chief of police never called me. He tried to avoid me as much as possible.

"What are you up to?" he demanded.

"Eating some Chinese takeout. Delicious stuff."

"Don't be cute. What were you doing at the historical society?"

I blinked. "How did you know I was there?"

"The woman who works there just called me. She said you were snooping around, looking into what Garfield had been researching. She read about the murder in the press and thinks you're the murderer."

"Oh dear. She was staring at me while I was reading. If anyone is a snoop, it's her. Quite an unfriendly woman."

"Never mind. I told her you were nosy. That's what I tell everyone."

"Excuse me?"

"You think your investigations have gone completely unnoticed? You're always poking around asking questions. This is a small town. People talk.

You've developed a reputation as the nosy newcomer."

"Small-town gossip is less important to me than solving a murder," I snapped. Inside, though, I felt less confident. I should have realized Cheerville was a gossip mill. In fact, I already knew that. People were always telling me how so-and-so didn't keep up their garden and such-and-such a person at the senior center hogged all the chocolate custard. It had all been so banal that I didn't think it could affect me.

"Thank you for the warning," I added. "I'll try to be more careful. Have you found out anything?"

"We're looking into it."

I rubbed my temples. This guy was going to give me a headache.

"So what have you been doing exactly?" I asked.

"We've been checking on why he moved to Cheerville. A couple of people at the country club said he mentioned having family in town and that was why he had moved here. Wasn't too specific, but he mentioned it during at least two different conversations, so it was obviously important to him. Thing is, we can't find any relatives. In fact, we can't find any close living relatives at all. He had an older sister who died many years ago. Neither the sister nor Garfield had any children. We're extending the search to cousins but so far haven't found any in this state."

"Have you found out any more about his movements?"

"He hasn't been around very long, so no. The country club appears to be the only group he joined, although he had taken an application to join the Cheerville Historical Society."

An application he never got to turn in. Poor fellow.

"Did he make any friends at either institution?"

"Not that we can see. There was a new members' mixer two days before he was murdered. He was invited but didn't go. Apparently, it's quite a boozer. I guess he heard that and decided not to tempt himself."

"Have you investigated Chief Running Horse?"

"Oh, you found out he sold Garfield a house here in town, did you? We looked into the transaction, and all of it is aboveboard. I don't trust Chief Running Horse, though. We've done some background checking on him. Can't find any dirt on the guy, but my police instincts say he's dirty."

"I'm glad your police instincts can detect the blatantly obvious."

I heard Grimal mutter something on the other

end of the line. After a moment, he said, "Have you found out anything?"

I could hear the reluctance in his voice, the mortal fear that I would one-up him once again.

A well-founded fear, of course.

I gave him the time and date that Garfield signed into and out of the historical society and said that I "happened to remember" the maître d' had a ledger with a guest list for the charity dinner. "You should look into that," I told him.

Instead of a sullen response worthy of my grandson when he was getting an adolescent hormone hit, I instead got a long burst of mocking laughter.

"Well, of course we checked on that!" he said before letting out another long laugh. "That's basic police procedure. We checked that first thing. You really should stay in your lane."

I flushed red. There was nothing I hated more than unearned arrogance.

"Have you made any progress narrowing down suspects?" I asked through gritted teeth.

"The list didn't indicate who was left-handed," he said.

"Very funny. Question some witnesses. Look for who was sitting near the back so they would have a good view of Garfield and could slip away unseen.

Look at the table arrangement. Talk to the waiters. You know, basic police procedure."

I hung up. Ugh, that man drove me crazy!

Why was it that arrogance was almost always inversely proportional to competence? My late husband was one of the most competent men I had ever met, and he had not a trace of arrogance. He had confidence and a self-assured air that made him a natural leader. He could step up to a squad of gung-ho Marines and, in a few words, get them to follow him anywhere. He never boasted and never lorded it over anyone. He didn't need to.

If only everyone could be like that.

I spent the rest of the afternoon doing more background work online, searching for anything about the victim that could hint at why he had been murdered. I came up with nothing. Detective work, like spy work, required patience. Sometimes, long stretches of intense work turned up nothing. As the sky grew dark outside, I called Albert. Maybe I would get lucky and discover he had found out something.

"Hello, Albert. It's your least favorite little old lady. Have you discovered anything?"

"Huh?"

"Did you find out anything about the man who

tried to buy a drink for Garfield?" I asked as patiently as I could.

"Garfield doesn't drink. He eats lasagna." The guy broke out into giggles.

It took me a minute to catch the reference. "I'm not talking about the cartoon cat, you moron. You've been smoking, haven't you?"

"Whaaaah? No, not at all. I'm just, like, chilling."

"Did you check the *Cheerville Gazette*?"

"Um, sure. Didn't find nothing."

"This is important, Albert. A man's dead, and the murderer is a member of your country club. He could kill again."

"Uh, yeah. I'll get right on it."

I sighed and hung up. This zombie was going to be no help at all. Why did I have to rely on help from amateurs?

A few minutes later, I got a call from another amateur. At least he wasn't an idiot.

"Hey, pretty lady. I had a very productive time at the country club. I think I have a lead on the murderer."

My breath caught. Could I be so lucky?

TEN

Octavian and I met at the Candlelit Lounge.

I had picked the place because it was quiet and exclusive, the kind of restaurant where the rich set from the country club would go.

I also picked it because it was somewhere Garfield had gone. Chief Running Horse had taken him there after he'd clinched the house deal.

It was one of those subdued, dimly lit spots with white tablecloths, wood paneling, and oil paintings so dark you could barely see what they depicted.

And yes, there were candles. Not enough candles, mind you. Octavian discovered that when he walked right by my table.

I had arrived first, asked for a table well away from the other diners, and sat down to wait.

Octavian came in a few minutes later, squinted

as he surveyed the room, then started walking around looking for me.

I felt tempted to call out to him, but no one in this place spoke above a hushed whisper, so I felt embarrassed.

He came to my table, looked right at me, then walked on.

"Octavian," I called, getting over my reticence. Immediately, several other diners turned to me and frowned.

Octavian turned. I waved. He squinted at me and drew closer.

"Oh, it is you," he said and sat down.

"It isn't that dark in here."

He gave me an abashed smile. "Age. My night vision isn't what it used to be."

Good thing I hadn't taken him on my late-night break-in at the country club. "So how did your investigations at the country club go?"

He had come straight from there. I could tell because he smelled of cigarettes. Octavian didn't smoke, but he had obviously endured the country club lounge just to help me with my case. What a darling.

"I suffered through many a boring conversation and inhaled enough secondhand smoke to kill an iguana, so I hope you appreciate this," he said.

"Of course I do. By the way, do iguanas require a lot of smoke to kill them?"

"Indeed they do."

"What have you found out?"

We were interrupted by a waiter coming to take our order. I ordered a steak. Investigations always gave me a hearty appetite. Octavian squinted at the menu for a minute and eventually gave up, ordering the same, along with a carafe of mineral water.

Once the waiter was gone, we got down to business.

"For a while, I turned up nothing. I did rounds of drinks with various people. Everyone was happy to welcome me, and that welcoming generally included alcohol. That's why I ordered mineral water just now. I'm still a bit tipsy. There was a lot of talk about business in the city. While most of the guys are retired, old habits die hard, and they're still looking for connections."

"Why would they be looking for connections?"

"Networking never ends for some people. One mentioned a son who wants to get in my line of work. Another asked if I knew a good estate attorney. It's all kind of a test, you see. They want to know if I'll be useful to them. I guess it was different with your job. People had their orders.

Everyone knew what everyone else was supposed to do."

"We had to make local contacts."

"Ah, so you know about networking. Anyway, after a couple of drinks, people started to relax and began to talk, mostly about poor James Garfield. It doesn't bother you that I mention his name, does it?"

I stared at him, baffled. "Why would it?"

Octavian looked uncomfortable. "Well, you know … it's the same first name as your late husband."

"Oh."

It hadn't even occurred to me. I thought about it a moment and realized it didn't make any difference. When you had seen as much as I had, little things like that didn't get to you.

"It's fine, Octavian. What did they say?"

"Oh, they said all the right things, acting shocked about a killing in their midst and concerned about the killer still being at large, but that was mostly for show. After a while, they revealed their true colors. Started joking about how he had refused all their drinks. One of the guys does great impressions, and he did an impression of Garfield acting all flustered as everyone drank around him. That got a good laugh."

"They were laughing about a man getting murdered at their own club?"

Octavian made a face. "Sad to say, yes they did. Of course, it all shook them up a bit, but none of them wanted to show it, and so they joked about it."

I nodded. Operatives in the field did the same. We all joked about the bullet that knocked our hat off or the bad guy who had done a funny dance as we shot him. It was a way to defuse fear. We never joked about one of our own getting it, though. The gentlemen at the country club lacked a certain *esprit de corps*.

"Did you meet anyone who fit the general description?"

"A few. I also steered the conversation around to cars. Mercedes are all too common in that bunch. This is going to take some more digging."

I pulled out my phone and showed him the photos of the maître d's ledger. Beside each name was a table number, and another page in the ledger had a drawing of the meeting hall with all the tables and their numbers. I told him about Albert and the man trying to buy a drink for James Garfield. Octavian listened, entranced, at my account of breaking into the country club.

"I knew I saw something in you," he whispered, putting a hand on mine.

"Don't get frisky," I said, my giggle undercutting any sort of authority I tried to put in my voice. "We have a murder to solve. Now look, Albert said the man sat near the rear. I would say one of these nine tables."

My finger traced a circle around the tables at the back third of the room. Some weren't very close to the door, but I figured it was best to cast the net wide.

"One of those is ours," Octavian said, "and there were no single men sitting at our table."

"There were the Prices, and then there was that other couple. The man looked like a doctor."

Octavian sat up straight, an eager gleam in his eye. "Oh yes, I remember them. As a matter of fact, he fits the general description."

"Hold your horses. He got there too late. He and his wife only sat down a few minutes before the speech started, and he didn't leave the table before I did."

Octavian deflated. "Oh. Good point."

"Don't worry, you're being a great help. So that leaves eight tables. Let's make a list of men who were at those tables, and then we'll do a Google image search for all their names, trying to match the physical description Albert gave us. If we don't get images, perhaps we can get other information like age or place of work."

"Sounds like a plan."

The plan had to wait until after a delicious yet horribly overpriced meal. After we were done, we went to have a coffee at the Tic Toc Café. I picked it because the noise would keep other people from hearing what we were doing. According to Grimal, I had a bad reputation as a snoop that I needed to live down. The café was also well lit. I needed Octavian to be able to see what he was doing.

We got a table in a far corner next to a handsome old grandfather clock. My companion, another handsome old grandfather, sat right next to it. We ordered two coffees, and Octavian pulled out a notepad and pen. I smiled. The notepad was new. He had obviously bought it as part of his sleuthing kit. Too bad he hadn't bought a deerstalker hat. He would have looked cute in that.

"All right," he said, acting very businesslike. "I heard a lot of names while I was there. Why don't you start reading out names, and I'll write them down. Then we can search for them online."

We wrote down all the names, getting a total of thirty-eight people, well over half the guests at those tables. It turned out most of the men hadn't brought their wives. Most likely, the ladies had suffered through previous speeches full of golf jokes and decided to get facials or give their poodles a perm or whatever rich ladies did. Three men, Octavian had met personally, and he said they didn't match the description, so that left thirty-five.

"I brought my—" Octavian got cut off by the loud ringing, clanging, bonging, and cuckooing of all the clocks striking nine at the same time. The grandfather clock next to poor Octavian was the loudest clock in the place, and the poor dear leaned away from it, covering his ears until the cacophony stopped. I could actually feel it vibrate my insides. Explosions did that too.

Once we could hear again, I said, "Do go on."

"I—"

A little bird popped out of a clock over my head and went, "Cuckoo! Cuckoo! Cuckoo!"

"You're late," Octavian growled.

He looked around, scowling at all the clocks as if daring them to interrupt him again. They appeared to be cowed into submission by this, because none of them made any more noise other than their incessant ticking.

"Anyway," he began again, "I brought my laptop just in case we had to do any internet research."

He pulled it out of a briefcase he carried. We cleared a space on the table and got to work.

It was a slow process. Some faces we found immediately, from either newspaper articles or pieces in business magazines or company web pages. Others were harder to find, especially those with common names. You know how many Bob Millers there are in the world? Plenty, and it took some time to narrow them down.

Finally, we had eliminated as many guests as we could. We were left with twelve names. Three of them had a close enough general appearance that they could be our man. Five more weren't very close, but we didn't eliminate them because I didn't fully trust Albert's observation skills and memory. Four more, we hadn't been able to get images of at all. Not everyone had a lot of information about them on the internet. I suspected these were older club members who had retired before making much of a digital footprint. I couldn't be sure, however, so I left them on the list.

Then we got creative. Octavian tried searching for websites that contained the names of both James Garfield and each of the suspects, but he came up with nothing. Then we looked for public records of past convictions for each name, and besides a couple of divorce notices, again we came up with nothing. I even checked to see if any of the men were members of the Cheerville Historical Society. You never know, maybe it was a crime of passion between two men competing for the hand of the stern schoolmarm. No luck.

At last, I leaned back with a sigh.

"It looks like we've done all we can for tonight," I said.

"Now what? We still have twelve men to pick through."

I smiled. "Octavian, in this line of work, sometimes you have to keep company with people you don't like, people a bit different than you."

"Oh, we may have had different careers, but I wouldn't say we're apples and oranges. Besides, I find you excellent company."

"I didn't mean me, silly. I mean Albert," I said.

"The stoned waiter crashing at the country club?"

"Yes. It's time we had a meeting of the minds with that boy, assuming he has a mind. We have to show him these images and see if he recognizes the man who ordered wine for Garfield. If not, he can still be a great help, assuming we can keep him off the weed for long enough."

Now it was Octavian's turn to smile. "Leave that to me, my dear. Leave that to me."

ELEVEN

By a stroke of luck, the next day was Albert's day off. He asked us to meet him at Dips 'n' Donuts, which I had to ask directions for. I had never heard of it.

When Octavian and I got to the address he gave us, I could see why. It was out on a county road, well past the city limits. A little building that looked like it had once been a gas station was painted with garish psychedelic colors. On the roof was a big tie-dyed doughnut, at least six feet in diameter, slowly spinning on the end of a metal beam.

"How do you tie-dye a doughnut?" Octavian asked.

"I have no idea," I said. The door opened, and a pair of twentysomethings slouched out, followed by a poof of marijuana smoke. "But I think we're about to find out."

"Do you think your friend invited us here as a way of making us leave him alone?"

"He's not my friend, and yes."

Marijuana was legal for medical use in our state for those who had a prescription from their doctor. Recreational use was still strictly prohibited, so I wondered how Dips n' Donuts managed to survive so openly without getting shut down. Even Arnold Grimal wasn't that incompetent.

I got my answer at the front door. A notice said, "Medical Marijuana Distribution Center. All buyers MUST produce their state permit for medical marijuana before we can sell to you. Peace."

Albert had a medical condition? Somehow, I doubted that.

We entered, and at first, I saw nothing because I broke out in a series of sneezes.

"Here, grandma," some dull-eyed kid in a waitress uniform said, handing me a surgical mask. I put it on. The sneezing subsided, and I got the chance to look around.

The dimly lit interior was fitted out like a living room, with sofas and easy chairs and bean bags. Most were occupied by young people smoking from pipes, joints, or bongs. Yes, I knew what bongs were. Just because I was old and disapproved of drugs didn't mean I was innocent. A side room had a set of gaming consoles that would have made my grandson moan with envy. All the chairs in that room were filled by young men staring at the screens through their bloodshot eyes, their fingers moving with remarkable dexterity over the controllers. Some soothing Asian music filtered through an invisible sound system. It sounded like Buddhist chants or old plumbing when you turned on the tap. Something like that.

To one side of the main room stood a counter where various brands of marijuana were on display on little trays. Behind it stood a middle-aged man with dreadlocks and a Phish T-shirt. He studied us through sober eyes. In fact, he was the only sober person in the room besides us.

Albert sat at a corner table, a joint between his fingers. He saw us and flashed us a peace sign, which made him drop his joint. It landed on his shirt, and he slapped it out before it could set him on fire. We went over.

"You have a permit for medical marijuana?" I asked as we sat down. He looked like he had been taking a lot of his "medicine" that morning.

"Yeah, of course. The dudes here run a tight

ship. They don't want the man coming down on them."

"What's your condition?" Octavian asked. Unlike me, he wasn't having a sneezing fit. In fact, he looked remarkably comfortable in this strange place.

"Um, like, glaucoma."

"What's glaucoma?" I asked. I knew very well what it was, but I wanted to see if he did.

"It's, like, an eye thing … right?"

"So your doctor gave you a permit?"

"Oh yeah," he said, chuckling. "Doctors are cool about that."

I bit my lip. Yes, doctors were all too quick in handing out medicine. So quick that the average lifespan of Americans was actually declining thanks to the overprescription of opioids. At least you couldn't overdose on marijuana like you could on opioids. The worst that could happen was that you ended up like Albert.

That was bad enough.

The young waitress who had given me the surgical mask came over.

"Can I take your order?" she asked. Her eyes were almost closed, not that I could see them very well under her blond dreadlocks.

"We don't need any marijuana," Octavian said. "We're just here to speak to my, um, grandson."

"No, I mean, do you want something to drink? We don't do table service for the marijuana," she said.

"Oh, um, an orange juice for me," Octavian said.

"I'll have a chamomile tea," I said.

When she left, Octavian turned to me. "She didn't look surprised to see us here. In fact, no one does."

Albert cut in. "Plenty of old people come here."

"You mean for legitimate medical reasons," Octavian said.

"I have a legitimate medical reason."

"No you don't. You're wasting your life."

"Hey, you're not my dad."

"If I was, you wouldn't be like this."

"Gentlemen," I said. "We have a murder to solve."

"Oh yeah, that," Albert said. "I checked out the *Cheerville Gazette* like you asked. No dice. I've been keeping an eye out at the country club too, but I haven't seen the dude."

"You probably did, but you don't remember," Octavian grumbled. "You probably don't remember what you did five minutes ago."

"Sure I do. I was, like, um …"

"Can we focus on the task at hand, please?" I asked. Octavian pulled out his laptop.

"Here," he said, opening it and turning the screen so Albert could see a mosaic of photos we had collected of country club members who had sat near the back during the dinner. "Is any one of these the man who asked you to give a drink to James Garfield?"

He studied each one. To my surprise, he appeared to actually take this seriously and focus on each face. At last, he shook his head.

"Nope, sorry. None of these is the guy. He kinda looks like him, though." He pointed at one man. "But the guy I talked to was thinner and had less gray hair."

"It must be one of the four men we couldn't find an image for," Octavian said.

I nodded. "That's something. I'll cross-check their names with the Department of Motor Vehicles to see if any owns a black Mercedes."

"They won't tell you," Albert said.

"Oh yes they will. I have my ways."

Albert laughed. "Disguises, guns, contacts in the government … you are one weird old lady!"

"Watch your tone," Octavian snapped.

"What?" Albert said.

"You should learn some respect for your elders, although I guess that won't be forthcoming considering that you don't have any respect for yourself."

"You sound just like my dad," Albert griped.

"No I don't. If your dad had told you these things, you wouldn't have turned out this way. Do you want to be a nobody for the rest of your life?"

I was surprised that Octavian cared at all about this chronic underachiever. After all, Albert wasn't his responsibility. But I had not yet finished getting to know my new boyfriend.

Albert waved his hand in a dismissive gesture and picked up his extinguished joint from where it sat on the table. "You don't know me, dude. I'm probably making more than you did at my age. The country club gig is just a cover, bro."

"A cover for dealing drugs." Octavian looked ready to smack him.

Albert laughed. "If it's legal for some people, why shouldn't it be legal for everyone?"

"I don't believe for a minute all these kids here have glaucoma or some other medical condition."

Albert gave him a smug smile. "Of course they don't. They jumped through the hoops to get a medical certificate, just like I did. Not everyone wants to do that. It's a pain, and then you end up on the Feds' list. A lot of people prefer buying it the old way. That's where I come in. But don't worry, bro. Uncle Sam gets his cut. I declare it all as tips on my tax forms. They got Al Capone for dodging taxes, but they ain't gonna get to me that way."

I was amazed he was confessing all this but then realized I had pretty much caught him in the act that night at the country club. Besides, it wasn't like we could prove anything.

Now I wanted to smack him.

To my surprise, Octavian gave him a warm smile and put a hand on his shoulder. From the look on Albert's face, he was even more surprised.

"You could have a great future in business," Octavian said. "You identified a demand in a changing market that wasn't being adequately served. You have obviously researched your product and consumers well and offer a reliable service at a price low enough that they don't go to the competition, namely this place. And you even keep your taxes in order. I've known many entrepreneurs who have fallen down on this last step. Some didn't even try to fudge their taxes. They were merely ignorant of the laws and either paid too much tax or paid too little and got in trouble. There's only one flaw in your business plan."

"What's that?" Albert asked. Octavian had his attention now.

"Your business isn't sustainable. Sooner or later, you'll get caught."

"I'm careful."

"Perhaps you are, but are all your customers careful? If one of them gets busted, the first thing the police will do is ask where they bought the marijuana. They'll offer to let them go in exchange for their dealer's name. Your name."

Albert paled. He obviously had never thought of that.

Again, there was a reason they called it dope.

Albert tried to rally. "They'd never do that. Most are my friends."

Octavian gave a sad smile and shook his head. "Every day, there's some poor sap in the newspaper who thought the same thing. And many of these dealers who get caught aren't peace-loving hippies like you. They're gangbangers who'd shoot anyone who squeals. People who command fear. And still people point the finger at them in order to save themselves."

Albert didn't reply.

Octavian squeezed his shoulder. "You're not dumb, Albert. Underneath all that fog, you're an intelligent young man. Someone who could make a future for himself. I'm not saying you have to be some boring old suit in an office building somewhere, but you have the entrepreneurial spirit. With a bit of training and focus, you could make some good money. You could do anything you want."

He produced a business card. He didn't do a sleight of hand like Peter and Penny Price, but it had a similar effect on the stoned young man. Albert blinked at it and cocked his head as he gingerly took it. Apparently, no one had ever offered Albert a business card before.

"When you sober up, call me."

We stood.

"Thank you for your help, Albert," I said. "It really brings the case forward."

"Good luck, son," Octavian said.

Albert sat there, looking confused.

After we got out of there, I removed my surgical mask and took a deep breath of fresh air. Then I gave Octavian a peck on the cheek. "That was quite a pep talk you gave him."

"The boy needed it. And I meant everything I said. If there's one thing I understand, it's business and people who have the potential for it. You saw how he focused on those pictures even though he was more baked than Grandma's apple pie? He's got a sharp mind. He won't for long if he keeps dulling it with that junk, though."

"Don't expect him to make the right choice. People so rarely do," I said as we got to his car.

"That's too cynical. I suppose given the kind of people you had to deal with in your line of work, you're used to seeing the worst society has to offer. But in the civilian world, people tend to bumble along just fine. Albert may never live up to his full potential, but I wouldn't be surprised if this was all just a phase."

"You're a dear."

"Can you be a dear and drive?" he asked, handing me his keys. "I think all that smoke in there got me stoned. I'm having trouble thinking clearly, and that tie-dyed doughnut on the roof is beginning to look tasty. As a matter of fact, can we stop at a bakery?"

TWELVE

A quick call to the CIA records office got an old friend there on the task of matching car ownership to the four names we couldn't match pictures to. The CIA had access to the DMV. I wasn't sure if they had actually been granted that liberty, but protecting the country meant we sometimes bent the rules or even broke them. Had that sometimes been abused? Yes, sadly, it had. For the most part, however, it had been a force for security.

My friend came up with nothing. None of those four names owned a Mercedes of any color.

I then asked her to go through the entire list of names we had, all thirty-five of them. She came up with seven matches, Mercedes being a popular vehicle. Four weren't black, so I discarded those, leaving three. Two were matched to men who didn't look a thing like the man who tried to ply James Garfield with wine.

The third was owned by the man who Albert said looked a bit like him but was too old and heavy.

That got me wondering. I went back to the source of that picture. It was a legal magazine article about Rob Fleming, a lawyer there in Cheerville who got in the news for winning a major case using a clever interpretation of contract law. I didn't understand the intricacies of the legal argument reported in the article, but that didn't matter. The man was obviously successful and no doubt very well off.

The thing that struck me was the date of the article—four years ago.

Rob Fleming's age as reported in the article was fifty-four, meaning he was fifty-eight now. Men in their fifties were strange creatures. I'd known many of them. Their midlife crisis had generally passed. It was men in their forties who tended to buy sports cars and trade in their wives for a newer model. They were passing out of their last glimmer of youth and desperately grasping at it.

Not so with men who'd made it into their next

decade. Generally by that time, especially for professional men, they were at the top of their game in their chosen field and had accepted the fact that they were what they were. Youth was gone, their kids had grown or were close to that point, and their main concern was the fact that they were aging. A lot of men got their first heart attack in their fifties. Some men even died from one thing or another. Men in their fifties began to get scared.

This led to one or two reactions—shrugging their shoulders and accepting that life had nothing more for them except a gradual downward slide or going on a health kick. My gym was filled with men in their fifties.

Had Rob Fleming gone on a health kick, getting rid of the extra weight and dyeing out some of his gray hair?

I scoured the internet for more images of Rob Fleming but couldn't find anything new enough to confirm my suspicions.

Until I hit pay dirt.

Two years ago, Rob Fleming gave a speech at a convention of the state bar association. A convention report on the bar association's online newsletter included a small and not particularly clear photo of Fleming standing at a podium and speaking to the assembly.

Yet the photo was clear enough to show that his hair was less gray than in the previous photo, and he looked like he had lost weight.

A halfway point between the man in the first picture and the man Albert had spoken to?

I emailed both pictures to Albert along with an explanation of my theory. To my surprise, he texted me back within a few minutes.

"Gr8 detective work, granie! Think ur rite. If the dude at the speach lost a few more and put in some hair die he'd be the dude with the whine. Ill try to find out more tomorow, brb."

Entrepreneurial potential or not, Albert needed to work on his spelling.

And I had to Google "brb." Turned out it meant "be right back." But of course he wouldn't get back to me until tomorrow at least. I guessed that in the stoner community, that counted as getting right back to someone.

I would have to be patient. This was not the sort of murderer who would be killing again. Even if it wasn't Fleming but some other "pillar of the community," the man had murdered for personal reasons. He was not some lunatic like the man who'd tried to kill the movie star Cliff Armstrong, someone who would slaughter a whole crowd in order to take out his target. Whoever killed James Garfield had done so on the sly, hoping to preserve whatever part of his life Garfield had put in jeopardy.

And what was that? The young woman in the photo? His daughter, perhaps?

No, not a daughter. One of the personal details I found was that Fleming had two sons. No daughters. A trip to the county records office did turn up that he had gotten divorced five years previously, however.

The following day, I got a cordial invitation from Octavian to lunch with him at the country club. Yes, he used "lunch" as a verb. He was really getting into this whole country club thing.

The lunch was more of a work meeting than a date. It turned out that there was a special lunch for members on the first Saturday of every month. "First Saturdays" were a long tradition at the club, and most members made a point of attending. We might just get lucky.

I felt grateful for him offering to drive. His Lexus was far more presentable than my Nissan, and thankfully, he had recovered from the second-hand smoke of the day before. I hoped his stomach had recovered from all those éclairs he had devoured on the drive home.

"I'm glad you heard about this," I told him as

we drove up that sweeping driveway to the plantation, um, I meant the country club. "This could be just the break we need."

"Actually, I had forgotten all about it until Albert told me. There's hope for that boy yet."

"So he actually called the number on your business card?"

"He did indeed. I was worried he would use it as a filter for one of his joints."

"Filter?"

"You put a bit of rolled-up paper, preferably hard paper like from a business card, at the end of the joint so you can smoke the joint all the way down to the end without burning your lips."

"You seem to know a lot about it."

"Here we are," he said, stopping in front of the parking attendant.

The lunch took place in the grand ballroom. It felt a bit eerie being back there. Octavian and I instinctively took a seat near the back by the doors so we could watch everyone come and go. Octavian was turning out to be a natural at this.

We scanned the room, looking for Rob Fleming. There must have been a couple of hundred people standing in the room and the front hallway, both men and women. It turned out more men had brought their wives this time. I hoped that meant there would be no golf jokes.

After we didn't see him for a few minutes and the room began to fill up, Albert appeared at our table, dressed in his white blazer with the logo of the country club on the breast pocket. So far, we were still the only people at the table, since there was no assigned seating and most people went to the front.

"Can I take your order?" Albert asked, acting normal as some more people filed past.

We ordered. Once the coast was clear, he leaned in and said, "I haven't seen him."

His eyes weren't bloodshot, and he spoke clearly. He seemed a far cry from the stoner we had spoken to at Dips n' Donuts.

"Are you sober?" I asked, unable to keep a note of surprise out of my voice.

"Of course he's sober," Octavian said. "He's got an important job to do."

Albert smiled at him. "Yeah. Don't worry. I'll keep an eye out."

He moved on.

"Might be getting somewhere with that underachiever," Octavian said.

"At least for today."

"Yes. If we catch the murderer, he'll probably

celebrate by smoking an entire shipment from Mexico."

We continued to scan the room. As it filled, that task became increasingly difficult. People gathered in groups between the tables, laughing and joking and generally obscuring the view. One annoying group stopped right between us and the doorway. They were barely in the room! It was like those people who walk into the supermarket right in front of you and stop just inside the front door and stare around them, blocking the way. Didn't these people know I was trying to find a murderer?

A moment later, I did find someone, but it wasn't Rob Fleming.

It was the woman in the photograph next to James Garfield's bed.

She was unmistakable, a blond woman in her late twenties, dressed to the nines in an expensive turquoise dress. She even had on the same diamond necklace and ring she had worn in Garfield's photograph. Accompanying her was a woman in her fifties who was just as well dressed and with equally rich jewelry. She was obviously the girl's mother. The family resemblance was visible even through the older woman's facelift and chin tuck.

They came in alone, greeting a few people as they passed our table. Several of the men made a point of coming over. The older woman and her daughter got similar attention. I suspected the mother was a widow with heaps of money and the daughter one of the more eligible single women in town. The way the men interacted with her, that diamond ring did not symbolize an engagement.

I nudged Octavian and pointed them out.

"That's the girl in the picture I told you about," I whispered. Still no one had sat at our table, but it was best to stay cautious.

"She's got at least twenty thousand dollars in jewelry on. Her mother has about the same."

I blinked. He had made that assessment with barely a glance.

He saw my reaction and chuckled. "When you hang out with rich people all your career, you learn to read the symbols. You have to show off your wealth in a communicable way in order to show where you are in the hierarchy."

"And how did you do that?" I asked.

He pulled up his sleeve and showed me a beautiful gold watch. "A vintage Rolex from 1926. There's a shop in London that specializes in vintage Rolexes, some reaching the high five figures. That combined with a tailored suit, and the business connections came pouring in."

"Well la-di-da."

"So what's our next move?"

I shrugged. "Introduce ourselves. You're the newest member of the country club, after all."

"The direct approach. I like it."

We made our way over to the women. Octavian expertly navigated through the small crowd of admiring men encircling the two ladies. As down-to-earth as that man could be, he really was in his element in this crowd. I followed in his wake.

"Hello," he said, extending a hand to the younger woman. "I'm Octavian. I just joined the country club a couple of days ago, and I wanted to come over and tell you that that is a stunning necklace. My late wife had one just like it."

"Oh, why thank you. My name is Gwendolyn," the girl said in a tone that showed she was accustomed to receiving compliments. Her eyes turned to me.

"This is my friend Barbara," Octavian said. What, I had been demoted to friend? His reasons became apparent a moment later when he turned to the older woman. "And this must be your daughter."

That provoked a tittering from the two ladies and a raised eyebrow from me. He stole that line from a movie. I couldn't remember which movie off the top of my head, but flirtation didn't have to be original to be effective.

And it sure was effective.

The older woman slid over to him and placed her hand in his. He duly kissed it, right on a giant ruby ring that, while smaller than the one Penny Price wore, was far more tasteful and probably more expensive.

"I'm Gwendolyn."

Octavian cocked his head. "I thought your mother was named Gwendolyn."

"She's my daughter, you charming man, and she's Gwendolyn III. I'm Gwendolyn II, and my mother was simply Gwendolyn."

Octavian raised an eyebrow. "You're carrying your given names down through the generations?"

"Why should only men get to do that? It was my mother who created the family fortune with a chain of boutiques, and she passed it along to me. My daughter will inherit in due time. She's already proving to be an excellent manager."

Well, well, well. Not only was the mystery woman in Garfield's photo a prize catch, but she was also a member of a dynasty. This was getting better and better.

Someone cleared his throat beside me —Albert.

"I've set your drinks on your table, ma'am," he said, looking significantly toward our table.

I followed his gaze and saw why he had interrupted us.

Rob Fleming stood just a few feet away from my seat, talking with another man.

I moved off from the circle a bit. Albert followed.

"You sure that's him?" I whispered.

"Yep."

"You sure you're sober?"

"Yep."

I glanced over my shoulder. Octavian was still chatting with Gwendolyn II, while Gwendolyn III was talking with a young admirer. A lot of them were circling around like fruit flies.

Just as I was about to head over to Rob Fleming and think of an excuse to speak with him, he wiped his nose with the back of his finger and headed toward us.

Wiped his nose. Cocaine users did that a lot. And he wiped it with his left hand. The autopsy had said the murderer had been left-handed.

He went straight up to Gwendolyn II, passing me without a glance. I moved back into the circle and stood beside Octavian.

Fleming's appearance made Gwendolyn II's

eyes light up, and a genuine smile spread across her lips.

"Darling!" she said, placing a kiss right on his mouth.

"How are you, my love?" Fleming asked.

"Much better now that you're here. Rob, I'd like you to meet Octavian and Barbara. They just joined."

There followed a superficial conversation during which I studied everyone's body language. Fleming and Gwendolyn II had hooked arms and stood so close their sides were touching. Fleming was polite to us but obviously uninterested. Gwendolyn III took time out of chatting with her young admirers to chat happily with Fleming. Everyone seemed at ease. Gwendolyn II might have been a good catch, but I didn't sense Fleming was courting her entirely for that reason. Her wealth might have been a bonus, but that wasn't his prime motive. No, this was a family in the making.

So what had happened to the older woman's husband, the father of Gwendolyn III? Dead? Divorced? He was obviously out of the picture, and I couldn't ask while lover boy was around.

Fleming coughed. "If you'll excuse me, I'll be back in just a minute." He headed for the door. I was about to follow when I saw Albert trailing him.

If Fleming was heading to the bathroom for another snort, it would be better if Albert went. The last thing I needed was to gain a reputation as the old lady who hung out in the country club men's room.

Then I thought again. If Albert snuck in there, he could get himself in trouble or even killed. Octavian was still chatting to the two Gwendolyns. Apparently, he hadn't put two and two together and decided to follow our main suspect.

Good. I didn't want him getting stabbed at the urinal. That would be a very sticky end, to say the least.

I walked away without saying anything, hoping to leave unnoticed. Octavian was putting on the charm, and Gwendolyn II was obviously interested in whatever he was saying. Gwendolyn III had turned away to speak with a new suitor. If I slipped away unobtrusively, no one would even know I had left.

Wrong. As I moved away, I caught Gwendolyn II glancing at me. A flicker of suspicion passed over her features. Her brow furrowed a little, quite a trick when you'd had a facelift. I didn't know you could furrow your brow after one of those.

Even worse, she saw me looking at her. Our eyes met for the briefest of instances.

I gave her an awkward smile and moved off.

"Keep that charm coming, Octavian," I said under my breath. Maybe he could keep her occupied and out of the way.

I trailed Albert out the door and down the hall. I couldn't see Rob Fleming because he was too far ahead, but Albert seemed to have him in sight. I sped up, my ankles hurting a bit. I clutched my purse, which had my 9mm hidden inside. I hoped I could clear all this up without gunplay.

The crowd cleared up, and I spotted Fleming. He had been stopped by some businessman who was eagerly talking to him about something. Albert stopped and busied himself, rearranging a floral display on a side table. I took the opportunity to move closer to Fleming while keeping behind him.

As I drew close, I heard the man who had stopped Fleming say, "So I think those stocks will turn a tidy profit."

"Sounds good," Fleming said with a nod. "That will put me in a good position."

"Wedding bells at last?"

Fleming smiled. "Looks like."

Wedding bells with whom? Gwendolyn II? There seemed to be chemistry there.

Fleming nodded in the direction of the bathroom. "If you'll excuse me, I need to hit the head before the lunch starts."

"Of course," the other man said, moving off.

I got close behind Fleming and followed. I had no fear of him noticing me. The man was walking with purpose, focused entirely on the drug he needed to take. I'd lost track of Albert in the crowd, but that didn't matter. I would handle this from here.

Fleming's hands were fidgeting, and his left hand kept straying to the side pocket of his blazer. His pace increased. This man didn't need the bathroom for any normal business.

He rounded the corner down the short hallway leading to the bathroom. For the moment, we were alone. Without looking back, he entered the men's room.

The ladies' room was just across the hallway. I glanced either way. No one was in sight. I forced myself to count to ten to give Fleming enough time to get into one of the stalls before I opened the door. When I did, I saw no one at the urinals but heard a telltale sniffing coming from one of the stalls.

Just then, Penny Price, of all people, came out of the ladies' room.

"Barbara, you silly goose! That's the wrong bathroom! This is becoming a bad habit with you!"

Good. Lord.

She caught me standing with the men's room door open. I heard a rattle inside, and one of the stalls opened. Rob Fleming poked his head out and looked right at me.

THIRTEEN

His eyes lit up, and I knew instantly that he had heard about the nosy old lady who had gone into the men's room to check out the murder.

The murder he had committed.

I knew that for sure now, because he struggled to maintain a calm demeanor while looking at me with a murderous rage.

Quite the emotion, murderous rage. I'd had it directed at me more times than I cared to count.

Luckily for me, he probably didn't have a knife on him, and a witness was standing right there.

"Barbara!" that witness said. "Close the door. You're embarrassing yourself!"

"And you're endangering me," I muttered.

Fortune favored the bold. I stepped into the bathroom and shut the door behind me, figuring that Penny Price wouldn't follow. The squawk she let out made it sound like she was right on top of me, though.

"You murdered James Garfield," I said, stepping forward and unzipping my handbag.

Rob Fleming's face did some impressive contortions. His first reaction was shock and fear, followed quickly by confusion over how I could know what I knew then by one of the best poker faces I'd seen in the business.

"You're crazy. Get out of here."

A knock came at the door.

"Barbara? What are you doing?" Penny Price called out.

"You tried to ply Garfield with wine, and when that didn't work, you watched as he drank his orange juice and then hid here in a stall until he had to relieve himself. On the way here, you stole a steak knife and used that to kill him. You were hyped up on cocaine, and so all it took was a single hard stab in the back."

More confusion showed on Fleming's face, followed by rage.

The cocaine had hit his brain.

If I had been thinking straight, I would not have faced down a murderer who had just snorted a controlled substance.

If he had been thinking straight, he would not have done what he did next.

He should have shouted that a crazy woman had broken into the bathroom. From an outsider's point of view, the situation did not appear in my favor.

But he didn't do that. Instead, he rushed me.

I got my gun out just in time. Fleming screeched to a halt a couple of feet from me, arms splayed out. I stepped to one side to get out of his reach. I tilted my head back so I could see the sights better. These days, I needed my reading glasses to see them properly, not that I had the time to take them out with him looming over me.

"How did you know so much about Garfield?" I demanded. "From what I heard, you never even met the man. So why did you want to kill him?"

Fleming's face contorted with rage. The cocaine was coursing through his veins now, hyping him up. I could see fear and anger battling inside him.

Just then, Albert saw fit to walk in. He really had bad timing. Why couldn't that young fellow learn to leave a woman alone when she was in the men's room doing some serious business?

"Whoa!" he said. "Looks like—"

Fleming grabbed Albert and threw him right at me. I managed to move the gun to one side so I didn't shoot the poor fellow as he crashed into me and sent us both to the floor.

Sharp pain lanced through my arm as I landed elbow first, then thudded through my entire body as the rest of me hit the floor. The gun skittered across the tiles.

Albert tried scrambling to his feet, only to get a right hook to the jaw that sent him down again. I rolled over and tried crawling for the gun.

"Tried" being the key word. My elbow felt like it was broken or at least fractured, and the fall had also put out my back. I didn't have back problems. It was one of the few parts of me that didn't hurt sometimes. *Thank you, Rob Fleming, for making me a little bit older.*

Not too old to trip him up as he went for the gun.

Tripping someone was an easy thing to do, even when you were prone on a bathroom floor with only one good arm. It just took timing. As he ran past, I grabbed at his ankle as he put his entire weight on it to bring his other foot forward.

The result was a satisfying face-plant on the bathroom floor and a sharp pain in my wrist. Great. Was I really going to have *two* bad arms?

It appeared so. I grabbed the gun and fumbled it, dropping it back on the floor.

Fleming, hyped up on drugs and rage, batted my hand away and reached for my gun, only to get a business card flicked right in his eye.

He cried out, and his hand went to his eye instead of the gun. Another business card hit him in the other eye. It came in fast and hit point first.

It couldn't have done any real damage, but it certainly must have hurt and blinded him for a second.

Long enough for me to get ahold of my gun.

When Fleming next got his eyes open, he was staring down the barrel of a 9mm.

No amount of cocaine was going to keep that from being a scary proposition.

"Is that you back there, Penny?" I asked without taking my eyes off Fleming. I didn't dare.

"Yes."

"That's quite the trick with the cards."

"I have plenty of tricks up my sleeve. Mind telling me what's going on?"

"This dude murdered a dude," Albert said, struggling to his feet.

"Prove it," Fleming snarled.

I paused. That might be difficult. After all, we had no physical evidence, nothing to directly link Fleming to Garfield. As for the drink he sent over to Garfield's table, he could merely say that he was offering the new member some wine. That was hardly evidence for murder. If we were lucky, he had some more cocaine in his pocket, and we could bust him for that. Then again, he could have me charged with assault. I was the one who barged in on him and pulled a gun.

Fleming gave me a wicked grin. He had thought of all this and probably lots more. He was a prominent lawyer, after all.

He let out a mocking laugh and sprang to his feet. I kept my gun on him, but with my other arm still in excruciating pain, I couldn't get up myself.

"Just as I thought. You're just some meddlesome old hag who thinks she's a detective. You and some dumbass kid and some nouveau riche wench with bad TV commercials. Some detectives! You have nothing."

"Yes we do," Octavian said.

I supposed he had dramatically appeared at the door at that moment. Too bad I had to cover Fleming and missed it. I did so love a man who made a dramatic entrance.

"What do you mean?" Fleming said, a little less confident than before. Something in Octavian's tone brooked no opposition.

"I was talking with Gwendolyn II and III, working on a hunch. I had asked around and found out Gwendolyn II is single, so that got me thinking about her ex. Gwendolyn II doesn't wear a wedding band like many widows do, like Barbara and I do. Divorce? That was my next hunch. So I got to talking to them and told Gwendolyn III that since she's such a lovely girl, her father must be very proud of her."

Fleming took a step back, shocked. Octavian let out a little laugh.

"Yes, that's the reaction I got from Gwendolyn II but ten times bigger. She turned pale and then got angry. Oh, she tried to hide it, but she couldn't. She must have heard things along those lines a hundred times, and she still can't control her reaction. Her daughter revealed even more. She said she had never known her father. That set off an alarm in my head."

It did in mine too. "James Garfield was the father. That's why he moved here, to be with her. That's why he took a photo of her. But he took it from a distance. Gwendolyn II wouldn't let him see his daughter."

"Why should she?" Fleming yelled. "That useless old drunk got her pregnant and left her. Even back then he was a drunk, and Gwendolyn's parents disapproved of him. They didn't want him in the family. And when he got her pregnant, he decided that his freedom was more important than responsibility and took off. Never sent money to help support the child either. Not that they needed it, but he should have been a man and offered. Then he shows up twenty-eight years later wanting to make amends? Gwendolyn was furious. It's better her daughter never knew her father than meet up with him."

"So you learned all about him from the woman you want to marry and killed him," I said as Octavian helped me up. What a gentleman. Octavian, not Fleming.

Fleming took another step back. "She didn't know a thing."

"I don't believe that," Penny Price said.

"Neither do I," Albert said. "No way."

Fleming straightened, obviously trying to get the rational part of his mind to gain dominance over the drug-induced emotions.

"You got me," he said in a calm voice. "But you'll never get her."

"We'll see about that," I replied.

FOURTEEN

Grimal didn't want me present for the questioning of Gwendolyn II. She was a major figure in town, and she had brought along one of Cheerville's prize attorneys.

Not Fleming. That particular prize attorney was in custody, awaiting a court date. Grimal held him on cocaine possession since he had some more in his pocket when the police arrested him. It was kept in a plastic vial identical to the one I found in the toilet. There was also the confession to murder he had made in front of four witnesses, although now, his lawyer was trying to wriggle out of it, claiming it was made under duress. It didn't matter. The police were gathering more than enough to convict him. His internet search history showed extensive research on Garfield, plus Chief Running Horse told police that Fleming had approached him at a bar one night, asking all sorts of questions about the victim. A couple of country club members said the same.

The prosecuting attorney felt confident Fleming would go to jail for first-degree murder.

I wished I felt the same confidence about Gwendolyn II. She came into the police station as cool as a cucumber. Unless they had been dumb enough to send each other emails or text messages about the murder, it would be tricky proving collusion.

Neither Gwendolyn II nor Fleming struck me as dumb.

Especially not the heiress. She was as cunning and ruthless as Fleming, minus the substance abuse. She'd been verbally sparring with Grimal for an hour now and had him on the ropes.

I stood in the observation room, looking through the one-way mirror and listening via the intercom to Grimal interrogating Gwendolyn II. He had gotten nowhere. My arm was in a sling thanks to a fractured elbow. My wrist and back didn't feel too hot either. I had told my son and daughter-in-law that I had fallen, which was true enough. Now they were getting all fussy over me about "my fall." The way they said it made it sound like I had gotten to a certain stage of life where falls were common and potentially dangerous.

If they only knew.

Gwendolyn II's tactic so far had been to throw her boyfriend under the bus. She said that Fleming was prone to snorting cocaine, and that sent him into rages. She further said that she often felt frightened around him. I had to admit she almost had me going for a while. It all sounded so convincing, if heartless. Would she really point the finger at Fleming when he could so easily turn on her? But on second thought, perhaps it wasn't such a risky move. He had maintained throughout his initial questioning that she knew nothing about it. Obviously, he loved her enough that he didn't want to incriminate her. If he changed his tune now, it would look like he was taking revenge on her for her statements to the police, and any decent lawyer could call all that into question.

Gwendolyn II gave some background on her and James Garfield's relationship. They had met when they were in their early twenties. He was a promising young man fresh out of law school who had been snapped up by a big legal firm. She was working in her mother's company and would eventually inherit it. They had fallen passionately in love, despite her parents' disapproval over Garfield's already heavy drinking. Gwendolyn II admitted that she, too, had been a bit of a partier in those days.

Then she discovered she was pregnant. During one of their drunken nights of passion, they had forgotten to use protection. She decided to keep the baby.

"I could never have an abortion," she said passionately. "Every life is sacred."

I didn't believe she thought that for a second, but she did put on a fine act.

Garfield took off as soon as she told him they were going to have a baby, getting a job in Cincinnati and never looking back. For a time, she pined for him, then she grew to resent him and later—bless her noble heart—forgave him.

But she didn't want him back. On two occasions, she hired private detectives to find out what he was up to, and the reports that he was drinking as much as ever convinced her she had made the right decision in putting the relationship behind her. She never told her daughter anything about her father.

And then suddenly, a few months ago, he called.

"I was so shocked I nearly dropped the phone," she said. "He called the office, which is a listed number, using the name of one of my business associates he must have learned about somehow.

When he revealed who he really was, I couldn't speak. I just listened as he went on and on about how he had never forgiven himself for leaving me. He claimed to have stopped drinking. He said he wanted to try again, that I was the one love of his life. He had never married, never had any other children, and now he was moving to Cheerville so he could be near his daughter. He didn't ask permission. He simply decided to waltz back into our lives as if he had only been gone for an hour to the supermarket."

That all rang true. Garfield's move did seem to have been rather sudden and unplanned. She went on.

"I finally got my voice back and told him I didn't want him to come, but he kept pleading. He wouldn't listen. I told him in no uncertain terms that he would not see me, and he would not see my daughter. He begged, cried, saying he had changed. Finally, I hung up on him.

"Then I heard through the grapevine that he had bought a house here in Cheerville. When he called again, I told him what I said before, but he kept insisting that we meet. At last, I relented."

"Where did you meet and when?" Grimal asked.

"We met in private, in Cheerville Municipal

Park. I wanted to meet somewhere out of sight to avoid any scandal."

"Did you go with anyone?"

"Yes, my chauffeur, Antoine. He's a black belt, you see. As much of a security man as a driver. I didn't know what to expect."

"And what happened on this first meeting?"

"He showed up sober, which surprised me, but he looked a mess. Red nose, bloated figure, nothing like the dashing young man I had fallen in love with all those years ago. He talked and talked and talked about how he had changed his life for the better, but I didn't believe it. He was obviously still drinking. Oh, he had managed to not drink that morning, but James had always been a functional alcoholic. That's not good enough for me. I don't want a man who leaves his responsibilities and gets plastered every night."

"Did he ask to see your daughter?"

"He did. Of course I said no. He begged, though. He pestered me so much I agreed to meet with him again. In fact, I met with him a total of three times. I have to admit I had grown curious. He managed to stay sober all three times, so I began to wonder if he really did want to change. I felt sorry for him. I never wanted him to come to harm."

I didn't believe that for a second. I kept waiting for the other shoe to drop. The problem was, Grimal had two left feet.

"Did Rob Fleming know about this? Did he say anything to you?" our esteemed police chief asked.

"He was furious. Oh, I knew I shouldn't have told him James had come to town. I told Rob not to confront him, to leave it alone, and I'd convince James to go away. I thought I had calmed Rob down."

She wiped a fake tear from her eye. I'd seen Saharan sand dunes wetter than those cheeks.

"So you met with James Garfield in Cheerville Municipal Park all three times?" Grimal asked.

"Yes."

"And your chauffeur can corroborate this?"

"Yes. Yes. He can."

"Can you give me the times you met with James Garfield?"

She nodded and gave precise dates and times, and my job was done. One of the meetings happened at the exact same time that Garfield was in the Cheerville Historical Society, with a signature and a neutral eyewitness to prove it.

I smiled and walked out of the observation room. There was nothing more I needed to hear. I would have a meeting with Grimal after Gwendolyn had gone and have him go over to the historical society and collect the ledger as evidence.

It was all over for her.

I would like to have said I felt triumphant. Justice had been served, after all, but as I walked out of the police station, I had a bitter taste in my mouth.

A man had tried to make good after a wasted life, had finally gathered the strength to turn over a new leaf, and he'd been stabbed in the back for it. Stabbed in the back by a man who had been motivated by love or greed or a mixture of both. It didn't really matter which. A cocaine addict had thought himself more deserving of happiness than a drunk, and he made the drunk die on the floor of a public restroom. And the woman they had fought over lied calmly to the police, stabbing the murderer in the back just as effectively.

The three were a property developer, a lawyer, and a businesswoman, respectable members of the community who ran historical societies and gave money to children's charities.

I'd met a lot of different types of criminal in my life—drug kingpins, arms dealers, corrupt politicians, homicidal maniacs—and no one had earned my contempt more than these petty rich people who would rather kill than see their desires interfered with.

Octavian sat in the waiting room at the front of the police station. He'd assigned himself my personal chauffeur until my arm was better and I could drive again.

The poor dear had been sitting there for hours.

He put his book down and looked at me.

"How did it go?" he asked.

"We got her."

He nodded. "Good." He knew enough not to smile. This was no great victory, only justice.

He stood. I was in his arms almost before he had a chance to open them.

"Tell me something good about the world," I said into his chest.

"The country club has agreed to keep mum about your involvement. They're not speaking to the press at all."

"More rich people protecting themselves. I said I wanted to hear something good."

"I'm helping Albert apply to business school."

I pulled a little away and looked up at him. "Really?"

"He wants to start his own chain of medical marijuana shops."

"Good Lord."

Octavian smiled. "One step at a time. Once he hits the books, he'll realize he can't smoke and study at the same time. A couple of years of not smoking and maybe his interest will settle on something else."

"Maybe your new contacts at the country club can find him something," I said as he escorted me out the door.

"Oh, I'm not going there again. There's nowhere I can go to the bathroom in safety."

"Stop being a wiseass and take me out to lunch."

"By all means, pretty lady."

He offered his elbow, and I took it.

ABOUT THE AUTHOR

Harper Lin is a *USA TODAY* bestselling cozy mystery author. When she's not reading or writing mysteries, she loves going to yoga classes, hiking, and hanging out with her family and friends.

For a complete list of her books by series, visit her website.

www.HarperLin.com